Praise for
SO YOU THINK YOU CAN BE PRESIDENT?

"This book is a must read for all 100 United States Senators planning to run for President. Of course that's an exaggeration. All 100 of us are already running for President. And we can all use Iris Burnett's wit and insight. *So You Think You Can Be President?* is required reading not just for those of us who have had the audacity to ask ourselves that question, but for everyone." —**SENATOR JOHN KERRY**

"At a time when Presidential campaigns have become too dull and the news media too negative, this book brings back the humor in thinking about politics and government—Mark Twain would have loved it."

—**NEWT GINGRICH**, author of the *New York Times* bestselling novel *Pearl Harbor*, and *Real Change: From the World That Fails to the World That Works*

"A brilliant book that also solves the budget deficit. If Presidential candidates have to pass this test, there will be a vacant McMansion on Pennsylvania Avenue. And do you know what houses like that are going for in Washington these days?" —**P. J. O'ROURKE**, author of *On the Wealth of Nations* and *Peace Kills*

"I've been running for President since 1984, and I was a total failure. Then I read this amazing book, and today I am the leader of the free world! At least that's what I tell people in bars."

—**DAVE BARRY**,
humorist, novelist, and author of
Dave Barry's History of the Millennium (So Far)

"This triumph of a tome is what would happen if the most brilliant nerd of a political consultant were to write a strategy memo after taking acid for a week—which all of them should do anyway. I haven't had this much fun since I was at the Stones concert in Memphis in 1975 and passed out after 'Honky Tonk Women.' Iris is a muse you can use!"

—**TOM OLIPHANT**, author of
Utter Incompetents: Ego and Ideology in the Age of Bush, and the bestseller *Praying for Gil Hodges: A Memoir of the 1955 World Series and One Family's Love of the Brooklyn Dodgers*

"Self-delusion binds all sane human beings together. It keeps us off street corners predicting the end of the world. The DNA of Presidential candidates instructs us to be slightly

more delusional. It keeps us in New Hampshire predicting victory. Iris and Clay broke the code."
—**SENATOR BOB KERREY**, President of the New School and former Presidential candidate

"Any book that suggests me as a Supreme Court Justice is a winner. I'd remove the blindfold from the Scales of Justice statue, equip the lady with night vision goggles, and put a bat in her hand. Clay Greager and Iris Burnett for President."
—**RANDY WAYNE WRIGHT**, author of *Dark Light* and the bestselling Doc Ford series

"Mother Goose insisted that Grimm take this test, and his scores were amazing—so he's decided to continue not to be interested in anything, start numbers of unsuccessful businesses, and hire Karl Rove, and he feels sure he can be the next President. Mother Goose will, of course, be Secretary of State."
—**MIKE PETERS**, Pulitzer Prize–winning cartoonist

"A stunning, sunny book. It may attract a new breed of Presidential candidate: one with a sense of humor."

—DONNA E. SHALALA,
former US Secretary of Health and Human Services

"Socratic dialogue, anyone? Sometimes the right question can just change your life. Well, probability's on your side with this provocative little book that has more moral and philosophical questions than I had to answer in twenty-five years of schooling (or thirty-five years, if you give extra credit for Hebrew school). Whether it helps you to pick the right party, First Lady, Chief of Staff, or position on drug benefits for seniors remains to be seen, but it'll undoubtedly convince you that you may have the stuff to be the next leader of the free world (or at least play the role believably in a TV miniseries)."

—DR. ALLAN JACOBSON,
Professor and Chair,
Department of Molecular Genetics
and Microbiology, University
of Massachusetts Medical School

"No one who intends to shamelessly pander to the frigid citizens of New Hampshire or waste the best years of their lives trooping around Appanoose County, Iowa, should be without this book. If Ross Perot had read this book, well, never mind . . ."

—**STEVE DALEY**, former political reporter for the *Chicago Tribune* and notable Washington political consultant

"All current and future Presidential aspirants: Put Iris Burnett on speed-dial! Her unvarnished and practical advice stands out in a field dominated by poll-tested pablum. She'll make you laugh all the way to the White House."

—**LINDA PEEK SCHACHT**, Chair, Department of Political and Organizational Communication, Emerson College

SO YOU THINK YOU CAN BE PRESIDENT?
E PLURIBUS UNUM

So You Think You Can Be President?

200 Questions to Determine If You Are Right (Or Left) Enough to Be the Next Commander-in-Chief

IRIS BURNETT &
CLAY GREAGER

SKYHORSE PUBLISHING

www.skyhorsepublishing.com

10 9 8 7 6 5 4 3 2 1

Library of Congress Cataloging-in-Publication Data

Burnett, Iris.
So you think you can be president? : 200 questions to determine if you are right (or left) enough to be the next commander-in-chief / Iris Burnett and Clay Greager.
p. cm.
ISBN-13: 978-1-60239-202-1 (flexibound : alk. paper)
ISBN-10: 1-60239-202-1 (flexibound : alk. paper)
1. Presidents—United States—Miscellanea—Juvenile literature.
2. United States—Politics and government—Miscellanea—Juvenile literature. I. Greager, Clay. II. Title.

JK517.B87 2007
352.230973—dc22
2007040684

Printed in China

To our beloved spices: Maxine and David; our incredible children: Jordan, Seth, Joyce, Todd Alan, Scott, Lisa, and Wendy; and our amazing grandchildren: Zachary, Taylor, Nichole, Todd Jr., Noelle, and Hailey, whom we hope will learn how important it is to participate in the destiny of our nation by voting for a President . . . and more importantly, all of whom passionately encouraged us never to be serious about anything—especially Presidential politics.

CONTENTS
(or Do Issues Give You a Headache?)

NOTE

The questions having to do with any issue area are not necessarily contained in any one specific chapter. It's the way the bureaucracy works so just consider it preparation for your new job.

SO YOU THINK YOU CAN BE PRESIDENT?
E PLURIBUS UNUM

INTRODUCTION

WHAT EXACTLY DOES the leader of five legislative branches, ten executive branches, twenty departments, ninety-five independent agencies, and the free world do at work everyday? More importantly, what should the President of the United States (hereafter referred to as POTUS, unless we forget to do so) know before she or he is elected? What do you know about the important issues the POTUS faces today? And by this we mean those critical problems and concerns you can't avoid even if you only read the White House morning briefing memo. Or don't watch television or read newspapers. Or only speak to the five people who'll tell you what you want to hear. Or don't listen to the Girl Scout who has managed to find her way into the Oval Office to sell cookies. The authors of this test, realizing the mental and physical limitations of the prospective POTUS, have designed a simple test to see if you (yes, you) are qualified to be the next President of the United States (see, told you we'd forget).

The questions are true/false, fill-in-the-blank, and multiple-choice. As this process may be too difficult for some test takers, we are allowing candidates one "lifeline" of their choice; whether it be a relative who may serve later as an intern or an intelligent friend you would consider for Chief of Staff. (The American people will feel better if they think someone in government is smart enough to actually know what they are doing.) There may also be trick questions. To avoid, any name-calling, finger-pointing, or nah nah ni nah nahs (remember, you will be working in Washington), the "trick" will be pointed out somewhere in the question. Finally, since you are trying to determine if you have what it takes to be the most powerful person in the world, you *must* use a pen. Using a pencil and attempting to change an answer will mean that you are incapable of real decision-making and will want to cater to a perceived majority view. (If you're this type of test taker, we suggest you run for a Congressional seat instead.)

Some helpful hints we can offer the potential Presidential candidate before taking this test:

- Think *before* you write.
- Study obscure Internet sites.
- Quickly read through the Constitution.
- Get yourself a discarded copy of the US government's "Plum Book."
- Remember what John Arbuthnot, the renowned writer and physician, said sometime between 1667 and 1735, "All political parties die at last of swallowing their own lies."

Once you've completed the test, the aspiring POTUS must submit the questionnaire to soyouthinkyoucanbepresident.com. Some-time in January of the year before you intend to run (or three to five years before—if you think there'll be fundraising issues or plan to have a questionable relationship), you will receive your score. You can then tally your score with the score sheet we've provided. And no, we're not going to make alternative career suggestions or give any information about how to find a good career counselor.

Before you begin the actual test, below is a surprise "just for fun" trivia section to see how mentally well rounded you are. Think of it as a warm-up for the more difficult sections to follow. If you don't know the answer, leave it blank. We don't deduct points for unanswered questions, just for incorrect answers (much like Washington). You will not need to find the answers, because once you are in office, you will have an intern to do that.

Before tackling the trivia section, make sure you know the following:

a. Your home or cell phone number and your legal voting address—just in case there is a question about where you will go into exile after the election.

b. How much money you are willing to borrow to get elected. (Will you put up all your worldly goods if necessary?)

c. Your party affiliation.

d. If there is anything in your past that's so embarrassing you have to start making up a story as soon as you've completed this test.

e. How you feel about living in a fishbowl.

1. Who was the only President to order an IRS audit of his Vice-President?________________________________

2. Which President felt so insecure with the Secret Service that he hired his own security team?________________

3. Which President was referred to as "Taco Belle" by his staff?____

4. Which Presidential candidate, after being nominated by his party, declined to accept that nomination? _________

5. Which Presidential candidate failed eleven times to win his party's nomination?_________________________

6. Which President filed an application with the Patent and Trademark Office to acquire the rights to the Presidential Seal?_______________________________________

7. Name the only President to use a "stand-in" when visiting China. __________________________________

CHECK YOUR WORK AND MAKE SURE YOU DIDN'T MAKE A FOOL OF YOURSELF.

TAKE A DEEP BREATH AND CONTINUE ON TO THE NEXT CHAPTER.

INCREDIBLY PERSONAL HISTORY

(Yes, It Is Our Business)

CHAPTER ONE

"WHO AM I?" Every person asks this question at some point in his or her life. In Presidential politics, it is extremely important to know the answer to this question before other people (namely, gossip hungry Americans and slick politicians) make your mind up for you. Before they begin assuming things about you, you should know who (and what) you are and be able to stand your ground against . . . well, pretty much everyone. If you have a strong sense of yourself, you will be better equipped to deal with any rumors the media can dig up.

Regardless of the personal cost, don't hesitate to answer the following questions honestly. The repercussions for even a little bitty lie (there will always be someone who knows that you fibbed) will forbid you from even discussing running for any office; including, but not limited to, President, Mayor, a Congressional seat, any school boards, or even green grocer (no sneers or snickers please, it's an important place for community interaction).

Remember, anything you share about yourself quickly becomes public information and can have serious (or dreadfully silly) consequences. While you're answering these intimate questions, think about some juicy, yet relatively harmless, tidbits about your life that you can divulge to the American public. Safe gossip is not like safe sex because one can still be fatal while the other is . . . well, never mind, they can both be fatal. Nevertheless, if it's executed wisely, safe gossip reveals information that will not damage your image—or, more importantly, your chances to win—but still makes you appear to be an interesting person with some (colorful) substance.

The first thing Americans will want to know is whether you are a Democrat or a Republican. Not that it matters to us, but it might make a difference to your prospective constituents. For some people (those who from an early age were diehard liberals or staunchly held on to every penny with a tight fist) this may be an easy question to answer. But if you are still undecided, the following story may help you decide your party affiliation.

POTUS
Training Exercise #1

A Republican and a Democrat were walking down the street when they came across a homeless person. The Republican gave him his business card and told him to come to his office for a job. Then he took twenty dollars out of his pocket and gave it to the homeless person. The Democrat was very impressed, and when they came across another homeless person, he gave him directions to the welfare office. He then reached into the Republican's pocket and gave him fifty dollars.

Now, have you made a decision?

1. Who was our wealthiest President?________________

2. Who was our poorest President?________________

3. How many weeks of paid vacation is the President authorized to have?________________

GO ON TO THE NEXT PAGE

4. How many Presidents have filed for divorce while still in office?____________________

5. Which President legally changed his name twice while in office?____________________

6. Which President was sued for nonsupport of an illegitimate child?____________________

7. Which President was treated for prescription drug abuse while still in office?____________________

8. Which President wrote his memoirs using a pseudonym?____________________

9. Which President revoked the statute that required each President to be evaluated annually by the Human Reliability Program staff at Walter Reed Hospital? __________

10. Which President won an Olympic gold medal? _____

11. How many Presidents have been cremated?_______

12. How many Presidents have been buried at sea? _____

13. Which President uttered the famous phrase, "I never met an ex-President I ever liked?"____________________

14. If you think you are a Democrat, which of the following statements best describes your political philosophy?

- ❑ **a.** You expect to retire and actually receive money from the US government.
- ❑ **b.** You believe personal injury lawyers when they say they make most of their money defending people who can't defend themselves.
- ❑ **c.** You think that supply-side economics refers to your dope dealer's stash.
- ❑ **d.** You are happy that Icelandic fishermen use harpoons, instead of guns, to capture whales.

15. If you think you are a Republican, which of the following statements best describes your political philosophy?

- ❑ **a.** You think Jefferson Airplane is a new discount airline.
- ❑ **b.** You feel that the government should be allowed to pass "moral" laws such as those banning gay marriages or censoring the Internet.
- ❑ **c.** You believe that donations to the Defense Department are like contributions to the USO and should be tax-deductible.
- ❑ **d.** You explained to your child that Oscar the Grouch chooses to live in a garbage can because he doesn't want to find a job or contribute to the good of mankind.

GO ON TO THE NEXT PAGE

16. What is the Democratic Party's major platform issue? Choose only one.

❑**a.** Self-medication for all veterans.
❑**b.** International worker exchange program.
❑**c.** Our homeless.
❑**d.** Immigrants.

17. What is the Republican Party's major platform issue? Choose only one.

❑**a.** Oil well platform.
❑**b.** Drilling oil platform.
❑**c.** Offshore oil platform.
❑**d.** Americanizing oil wells in Middle Eastern countries platform.

18. A recently released anecdotal survey confirmed that 80 percent of Democrats stay up after the 11:00 news, while 90 percent of Republicans go to bed at 9:00, right after reruns of *Law & Order: SVU*. Which of the following choices best explains why?

❑**a.** Watching the 11:00 news is better than watching reruns of *JAG*.
❑**b.** The *Law & Order* doink-doink is inspirational and demonstrates thinking out of the box.

❑**c.** Mom and Dad thought it was a reasonable hour (and they always know best).

❑**d.** Going to bed at 11:00 demonstrates the "you have no power here" rebellion against parental authority.

19. When did you decide you wanted to be the President of the United States?

❑**a.** Your fellow classmates elected you to a high school office and you went from a boring geek to an influential stud.

❑**b.** After college, when your parents told you to find something to do or take some education classes to fall back on.

❑**c.** During the ride to your senior prom, you realized staying in the comfort of your limo was preferable to joining the masses outside.

❑**d.** After you saw *History of the World: Part I*, you realized that being President was the closest you could come to being king.

20. If you're standing on the corner of Connecticut Avenue and K Street, which way would you walk to get to your office?

❑**a.** North, toward the lobbyists who can help you with some issue, that is of relative unimportance

GO ON TO THE NEXT PAGE

(except to their clients, who may donate to your next campaign).

❑ **b.** South, toward the Lincoln Memorial to find inspiration before you make any world-changing decisions.

❑ **c.** West, toward the State Department, where you can find a million different ways to say nothing about everything.

❑ **d.** East, toward Dulles airport (taking the circuitous route) where you could board a plane and be anywhere else for the next four years.

21. Do you think people in Congress are worth more than $1,500 per year? (This was the salary that Congressmen made in the 1800s.) ______________________________

22. Do you think they should be paid only for the days they participate in votes or Congressional business? (This does not include fundraising activities for themselves or for their pals.) ______________________________

23. If you had a choice about how much money you could take home before taxes, which of the following would you choose to receive? (This could be a trick question.)

❑ **a.** $175,700—The highest salary of a government employee.

❑**b.** $400,000—The present salary of the President of the United States. (Plus the many perks the President enjoys.)

❑**c.** $175,600—The highest salary of a Congressperson.

❑**d.** $203,000—The salary of a Congressional leadership member. Plus the cost of living increases, political action committee earnings (which they can use), and all the free gifts and services they receive but can deny later on—if they are careful about accounting, e-mails, and trusted employees. (This is quite a leap from the early days when, during the Constitutional Convention, Benjamin Franklin suggested they go without pay. You can imagine the uproar that caused.)

For extra credit, with a promise never to disclose your answer:

24. Do you currently pay your taxes—without using a system of creative accounting or hiring an accountant who gets paid to be creative? (This may be part of the trick.)________

25. If you have to pay taxes, which of the following will you still be able to afford to pay?

❑**a.** Your heat, electric, and grocery bills in that big house at 1600 Pennsylvania Avenue.

❑**b.** Dinner and a movie with old friends. (And by this, we don't mean a night in your personal screening room catered by the White House Mess.)

❑**c.** A trip to some exotic location without using Air Force One. (Or taxpayer money for the hotel, food, and a good massage.)

Yes, that was a trick question! You know damn well that as President you can do whatever you want at the expense of your industrious taxpayers. And if you're smart (or perhaps, just plain lucky), you can live on the perks and put off buying anything on your own for eight years.

26. If you don't pay taxes, you'll use this financial windfall to:

❑**a.** Help the poor, the infirmed, and the needy.

❑**b.** Take lengthy vacations to remote places the news media can't find.

❑**c.** Learn a skill to fall back on after you leave office. (FYI . . . screwing up traffic whenever you go and making decisions that will affect the country for years after you're gone are not actually skills.)

❑**d.** Make the Treasury build a guest home for your friends.

27. If you are a Democrat, please look at the following list and choose five taxes you think should be increased in order to help the economy. If you are a Republican, look at the same list and determine the five taxes that should be cut in order to help the economy:

- ❑**a.** Accounts Receivable Tax.
- ❑**b.** Building Permit Tax.
- ❑**c.** Capital Gains Tax.
- ❑**d.** CDL License Tax.
- ❑**e.** Cigarette Tax.
- ❑**f.** Corporate Income Tax.
- ❑**g.** Court Fines.
- ❑**h.** Dog License Tax.
- ❑**i.** Federal Income Tax.
- ❑**j.** Federal Unemployment Tax.
- ❑**k.** Fishing License Tax.
- ❑**l.** Food License Tax.
- ❑**m.** Fuel Permit Tax.
- ❑**n.** Gasoline Tax.
- ❑**o.** Hunting License Tax.
- ❑**p.** Inheritance Tax Interest Expense.
- ❑**q.** Inventory Tax.
- ❑**r.** IRS Interest Charges.
- ❑**s.** IRS Penalties.
- ❑**t.** Liquor Tax.
- ❑**u.** Local Income Tax.

GO ON TO THE NEXT PAGE

- ❑ **v.** Luxury Taxes.
- ❑ **w.** Marriage License Tax.
- ❑ **x.** Medicare Tax.
- ❑ **y.** Property Tax.
- ❑ **z.** Real Estate Tax.
- ❑ **aa.** Recreational Vehicle Tax.
- ❑ **bb.** Road Toll Booth Taxes.
- ❑ **cc.** Road Usage Taxes.
- ❑ **dd.** Sales Taxes.
- ❑ **ee.** School Tax.
- ❑ **ff.** Septic Permit Tax.
- ❑ **gg.** Service Charge Taxes.
- ❑ **hh.** Social Security Tax.
- ❑ **ii.** State Income Tax.
- ❑ **jj.** State Unemployment Tax.
- ❑ **kk.** Telephone Federal Excise Tax.
- ❑ **ll.** Telephone Federal, State, and Local Surcharge Taxes.
- ❑ **mm.** Telephone Federal Universal Service Fee Tax.
- ❑ **nn.** Telephone Minimum Usage Surcharge Tax.
- ❑ **oo.** Telephone Recurring and Nonrecurring Charges Tax.
- ❑ **pp.** Telephone State and Local Tax.
- ❑ **qq.** Telephone Usage Charge Tax.
- ❑ **rr.** Toll Bridge Taxes.
- ❑ **ss.** Toll Tunnel Taxes.
- ❑ **tt.** Traffic Fines.

❑**uu.** Trailer Registration Tax.
❑**vv.** Utility Taxes.
❑**ww.** Vehicle License Registration Tax.
❑**xx.** Vehicle Sales Tax.
❑**yy.** Watercraft Registration Tax.
❑**zz.** Well Permit Tax.
❑**aaa.** Workers Compensation Tax.

NOTE

That was an awfully long set of answers for such a short question but remember these long-winded answers to simple questions may very well mirror what your morning Presidential briefings will be like.

28. You are aware that there are many hidden perks that come with the office of President. The one most attractive to you is . . .

❑**a.** You've always wanted to ride in a limousine with TV and free phone service.
❑**b.** You've always wanted to throw out the first pitch at a ballgame.
❑**c.** You really like the idea of being surrounded by at least six macho men who have guns, wear sunglasses, and say yes sir/madam to whatever question you want confirmed.

POTUS
Training Exercise #2

Most folks are dying to get a glimpse inside of 1600 Pennsylvania Avenue, whether to innocently nose around the President's personal quarters or to not-so-innocently survey the area. While security measures protect the POTUS from star-struck tourists and angry citizens, they hardly insure the big chief's safety. Everyone knows that if someone is desperate enough to kill the President, they will somehow find a way to do it. (Although this is only spoken about in speculative, and usually veiled, conversation.) However, an assassination attempt would probably not occur at the White House, where there are armed helicopters circling around every ten minutes, sharp shooters on the roofs of all surrounding buildings, street cops dotting the perimeter, and those horrible "do not back up" spikes in the drive-thru. The White House is no

longer accessible to the public and now even the streets directly surrounding it have been closed. But do you really want to assume that you are safe within the White House walls?

Security is something to enjoy, not to fret about. Think about it. You get to shop unencumbered by other buyers. You get to close airports if you are late or simply not in the mood to fly. You can scare the hell out of unsuspecting drivers as your motorcade forces them off the road. And you can inconvenience millions of people by tying up traffic in big cities even during rush hour. These are some of your perks. Besides, you are going be a great President—well prepared, honest to a fault, everyone's friend and ally. No one will ever want to hurt you. But we digress. What is important to know is that 1600 Pennsylvania Avenue is no longer an oasis in the center of the city. It is more like the "Little House on the Prairie."

29. With regard to your residence, if you had a choice would you:

❑**a.** Put up heavy-duty security fences so that no one could possibly even know the Casa Blanca was there.

GO ON TO THE NEXT PAGE

- ❑ **b.** Move the house from 1600 Pennsylvania Avenue to a place no one would ever want to visit. (Say, the suburbs in Virginia or Maryland.)
- ❑ **c.** Open the doors to the public and let them walk the halls, peruse the entertainment space, and use the bathrooms without actually sitting on the toilet seats. (Or at least covering them with some kind of tissue.) This way, you demonstrate your generosity without exposing the staff and family to diseases.

30. Since you long to lead the free world, can you identify which parts of the earth can rightfully claim the designation of free world?

- ❑ **a.** The Arctic Circle.
- ❑ **b.** A Target parking lot.
- ❑ **c.** Beijing (in their press releases).
- ❑ **d.** Non-pornographic Internet sites.

FACTOID: The Lincoln Bedroom is still heated by wood burning furnaces.

31. Choose one of the following that best describes who you are in terms of geography, an emotion, or a food type.

❑**a.** Your hunger for a Hamburg or maybe a schnitzel.
❑**b.** You yearn to eliminate all possible pandemic poultry.
❑**c.** You thirst for a dinar you can enjoy with a stiff drink.

Needed to deliberate on that one? We hope it didn't take too much out of you. Unfortunately, the media insists that the public know who you think you are, as well as who you want to be. This next question is similar but even more complex. We will consider giving you extra credit because of the degree of difficulty.

32. If you had to choose among the following campaign slogans (we won't use names but we will tell you that they've been legitimately used in the past by political opposition teams), which slogan would your opponent use to describe you?

❑**a.** Hey—your tie is open.
❑**b.** Hey—your eye is open.
❑**c.** Hey—your lie is open.
❑**d.** Hey—your fly is open.

GO ON TO THE NEXT PAGE

33. By law, you have to leave office after two terms. But what if you could create a loophole that would allow you to stay longer? Which of the following would you opt to do?

- ❑**a.** Declare a national state of emergency so you could stay on as Commander-in-Chief during this crisis. (Something like you discovered that Texas had nuclear weapons and was planning to secede to become part of Mexico.)
- ❑**b.** Announce that you have a terminal illness and you want the Make-a-Wish Foundation to grant you one more term in office.
- ❑**c.** Start a world war and then surrender to the enemy with the condition that you remain in control with the title Ayatollah Big Dog.
- ❑**d.** Have one of your covert operatives get access to the Presidential Physical Fitness Test and modify it so absolutely no one else could qualify. Without any other qualified candidates, you'll have to stay in office until they find one. (Which could take decades, if your operative continues to modify the test.)

What would you be willing to do to become President? (This is where you scream, "Anything! Anything at all!") Let's pause here for a minute so you can take a breath. This test can be exhausting, so take a moment before you proceed because the next part of the test gets even more exciting and personal. We can assure you, however, that these results will never ever, ever, ever be released to anyone (except maybe a company that really needs the information for product placement).

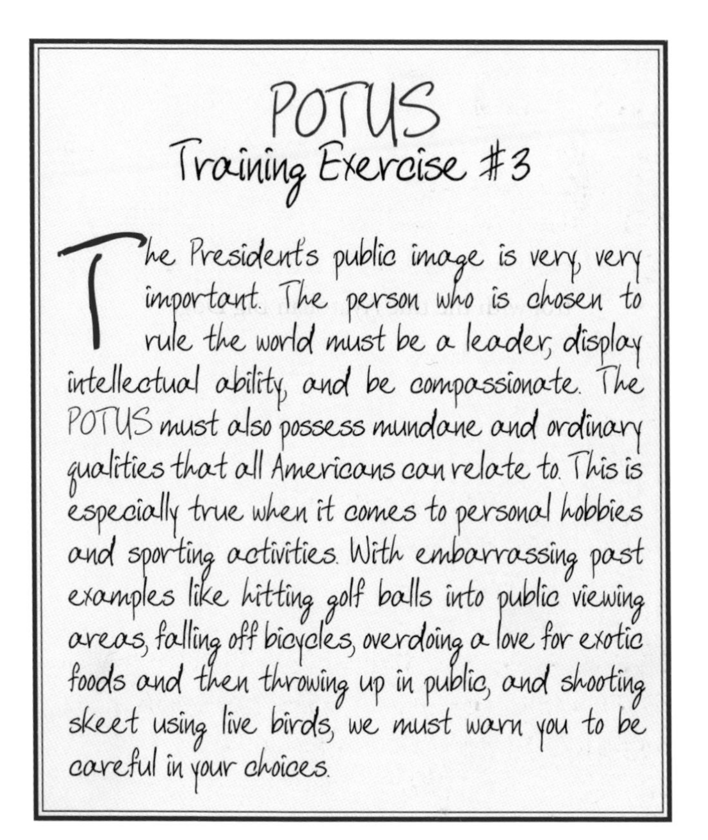

POTUS Training Exercise #3

The President's public image is very, very important. The person who is chosen to rule the world must be a leader, display intellectual ability, and be compassionate. The POTUS must also possess mundane and ordinary qualities that all Americans can relate to. This is especially true when it comes to personal hobbies and sporting activities. With embarrassing past examples like hitting golf balls into public viewing areas, falling off bicycles, overdoing a love for exotic foods and then throwing up in public, and shooting skeet using live birds, we must warn you to be careful in your choices.

Are you rested yet? Then let's continue with more personal gossipy questions. The public loves gossip and if you are willing to feed them good gossip, they will love you.

34. Presidents can't look weak or scrawny. Do you have a personal physician you can bring to the White House who can and will prescribe steroids? (It's important to look powerful and dapper for your press releases. Remember, there is no law requiring testing the President for performance-enhancing drugs.) ______________________________

35. Would you consider cosmetic surgery? (Fuller lips and arched eyebrows will send a hidden message to the gay community, which may be essential if you intend to run for a second term.) ______________________________

36. Which activity do you think would fit you best and still project an image of skill and confidence? Please choose from the following:

- ❑ **a.** Flying model airplanes into large buildings as an indication that you are not above doing the same with real planes against unfriendly nations.
- ❑ **b.** Speaking at evangelical fundraisers to promote Christianity in Tibet, Haiti, Somalia, and other like-minded countries.

❑**c.** Directing and producing home videos of guests who sleep over at the White House. Then having private showings to solicit funds for your next campaign.

❑**d.** Learning to play a five-string banjo and touring with the Rolling Stones. (You'd certainly capture four generations and keep alive that old axiom, "Sex, drugs, and rock 'n' roll!")

NOTE

Every modern President (except Eisenhower) has used some form of cosmetic enhancement. Good makeup and hair coloring does not seem to have a negative impact on the public perception of the POTUS or imply that the POTUS isn't working hard enough. Instead, it keeps the public from thinking that their fearless leader is about to drop dead from making too many ridiculous decisions.

FACTOID: The White House lawn is actually artificial turf and requires spray-painting once every five years.

GO ON TO THE NEXT PAGE

37. On the other hand, would you consider letting your hair naturally turn white? The public always notices this and makes them feel more compassionate towards you. If you go this route, remember to always use a lot of sun block when you're outside. They will be more willing to believe that you are a hard-working President if you are pale and sallow. If the sun block doesn't work you can have the doctor contact Michael Jackson's dermatologist (an additional perk is that you can contact anyone and they will take the call) to find out what he uses to lighten his skin.________

38. Choose two from the following books (which may or may not exist) that you think you should read before the inaugural.

- ❑**a.** *Feel the Fear and Do It Anyway* by Susan Jeffers.
- ❑**b.** *Au Contraire: Figuring Out the French* by Gilles Asselin and Ruth Mastron.
- ❑**c.** *GenderQueer: Voices from Beyond the Sexual Binary* by Joan Nestled.
- ❑**d.** *Decision Making* by Mark Anthony and Cleo Pat-Her.
- ❑**e.** *The Mafia Manager: A Guide to the Corporate Machiavelli* by V.
- ❑**f.** *The 21 Indispensable Qualities of a Leader: Becoming the Person Others Will Want to Follow* by John C. Maxwell.
- ❑**g.** *Terrorists and You* by Mustafa Levine.

39. Let's see if you can be as smart as the people who will make your life miserable. Here are some answers you might give to the media or, God forbid, the public. Please write appropriate questions for the following answers:

- ❑**a.** As soon as the Secretary comes out of his coma, I'll ask him.
- ❑**b.** Hell, I don't even know those people.
- ❑**c.** Of course I love going to church. There's a lot more to it than just playing bingo, you know.
- ❑**d.** They can't help it. Once they draw their pistols, they have to pull the trigger.
- ❑**e.** Just because they thought it was right, doesn't mean it wasn't wrong.
- ❑**f.** Well, it's true. Without experience, all one can do is give advice.
- ❑**g.** Save that one for next time.
- ❑**h.** That's not true. I change my mind all the time. I just don't tell anyone.
- ❑**i.** What do I look like? A used-car salesman? . . . Wait, I didn't mean it like that. Used car salesmen are honorable people. I apologize for saying that.
- ❑**j.** Sure, it costs a lot. I guess we'll just have to have the Treasury Department hire some part-timers to keep the presses running.
- ❑**k.** You don't see me worrying about my Social Security, do you? Besides, once we cut back on the

Medicare program, most people won't live long enough to collect anyway.

❑l. I'll give you the truth—as soon as I leave office and write my memoirs.

❑m. Yes, I am setting up a Web site so anyone in the world can sign on and join me for a weekly spiritual healing live chat. Just sign on to www.youremyidol.com. Of course, there will be a slight fee; idols don't come cheap.

❑n. No, I didn't say yoga would save the world. I said Yogi was one of our best marketing campaigns to save the forests. Who is yoga?

❑o. Give me your sick, your lame, your homeless, and I'll rebuild any city that has been destroyed.

❑p. Why don't I do more to conserve energy? How about I turn off the air-conditioning in this room, would that satisfy you?

❑q. Yes, it's difficult to find any private time where I'm not being hounded by reporters. You know, Elvis had the same problem. So there are special occasions when I go out and hide my identity by using, uhh, what do you call it, um, a pseudonym or is it a synonym? No, I think it's a cinnamon. Anyway, I had business cards made up with several different names.

❑r. No, I'm not concerned with getting an electric shock from the battery pack that supplies power to the receiver in my ear. It's always grounded to my balls. Does that answer your question?

❑s. It works for me!

❑t. It came to me in a vision one night while I was swimming naked in the White House pool.

❑u. Like the song says, "You got to know when to hold them, know when to fold them."

❑v. After a while I think everybody gets a little tired of giving and wants something in return for themselves. Right?

❑w. Congressmen and Senators are just like cattle barons. All they're concerned about is how big their herd is.

❑x. We really did screw up on that one . . . but don't quote me.

❑y. If the Chinese start exporting their cars into the US, all we'll see on the windows is a bunch of hieroglyphic scribbling followed by high numbers. How in the hell are we going to know what that means?

❑z. I can tell you this, in the year two thousand and sex, I'm going to take a hard stand on the declining morality that is penetrating our country. What? Did I say something wrong?

By the way, have you noticed the "factoids" we've included within the chapter? Hopefully you did because it's important to have a President who notices little details that can be easily overlooked. (Of course interns can do the noticing for you, but that wouldn't be the same, now would it?) To provide you with some relief from the rigorous test questions, we've interspersed them throughout each chapter.

FACTOID: The Electoral College is the only accredited institution not to have any members and grants only one diploma every four years, whether or not the recipient has passing grades.

CHECK YOUR WORK AND MAKE SURE YOU DIDN'T MAKE A FOOL OF YOURSELF.

TAKE A DEEP BREATH AND CONTINUE ON TO THE NEXT CHAPTER.

WILL THERE BE COLORFUL FAMILY SURPRISES?

CHAPTER TWO

THIS PART OF the test will give you an opportunity to look at the characters who share your blood and, more importantly, those who share your bed. It will help you to decide if your loved ones are really up to the job of first lady, brother, mother, cousin, dog, or cat. It may be easier to run as an only child with parents in an elder-care facility, but if you're stuck with an oh-so-colorful family like most of America, you'll need to think hard about all the stupid things they might do, or have already done, to embarrass you.

Family image is important to Americans. They want to know who has raised you and who was raised alongside you. However, the person that the public will be most interested in is your spouse. Unfortunately, you can't choose your family, but you can choose your life partner. (Most of the time, anyway.) You'll need to think carefully about the kind of "first" you want your spouse to "seem" to be and what type of image you'd like your spouse to emulate. (By

the way, using the term "first spouse," is our politically correct way of expressing our hope that some woman out there may actually have a shot at becoming "the man.")

40. Which of the following choices would you consider when selecting (or grooming) a spouse?

- ❑**a.** Personal wealth. (Although, if they have more money than you do, it's possible that you'll constantly be hearing, "Why don't you get a job that pays more?")
- ❑**b.** An illiterate spouse, illustrating the need for the "No Child Left Behind" program.
- ❑**c.** A person who is devoutly religious (if you are reading between the lines, this is an important quality for the POTUS because this implies that they will be forgiving. If you plan on having many interns, this would be an essential quality for your spouse to have).
- ❑**d.** Selecting a horse instead of a spouse.

41. How important is it to you to have a spouse who always looks adoringly at you?

- ❑**a.** Very important.
- ❑**b.** Somewhat important.
- ❑**c.** Not important at all.

42. If you believe your spouse should have a career, please choose the most ideal one from the following:

- ❑**a.** A lawyer. Preferably one who'll prevent you from getting into trouble. And, if necessary, one who is able to defend you when you choose to ignore his or her advice.
- ❑**b.** A doctor. Preferably a psychiatrist who can figure out the motivation behind what you are thinking when you make outlandish decisions. Plus, they'll be able to confuse the media and the public with convoluted medical rhetoric.
- ❑**c.** A candlestick maker. Someone who can help you find the light. Or shine the light on you. Or light your way. Or light your fire. If this is getting too esoteric, please move to the next question.

If you don't think your spouse should have a career, let us ask you this: Just who do you think you are, you selfish, unfeeling, arrogant, self-centered son of a (Oops. We may have overreacted just a bit. I suppose you've figured out our stance on this topic.)?

43. Do you have a brother or a sister who has ever been in jail?____

GO ON TO THE NEXT PAGE

44. You don't know? Okay, well, if they committed a felony, how serious was it? Did they:

❑**a.** Steal from the donation box?
❑**b.** Kill a cop?
❑**c.** Protest in front of the World Bank?
❑**d.** March in a gay rights parade as an Arabian princess?

45. How many children do you have? If you don't have children, then how many pets do you have? (If you don't have children, you have to have pets. You need to have something to which the public can relate.)___________

46. How many holes do your children have in their body? How many are self-inflicted? (Maybe using piercings is a better way to word the question—but still, holes are holes.)

____

47. Can you explain each of the piercings? When the media asks why your kids have holes in their tongues or navels, can you provide an explanation in a single sentence? Which of the following sentences would you choose as an explanation?

❑**a.** Ventilation is good for circulation.
❑**b.** Experiencing bodily pain is good practice for wars or for childbirth.

❑c. It was either that or a tattoo of the FBI's most wanted.

48. Have any of your children been arrested for drug or alcohol related crimes? Do they want to be?___________

49. Do you have any illegitimate children? (If you're a woman, you probably know the answer to this question. If you're a man, think back. Your opposition will have this information, so you should too.)__________________

50. The media and Christian Right will want to know your thoughts about legitimate children. What will you say?

❑a. An illegitimate child costs only a fraction of what it costs to raise someone who thinks they are legitimate. I know this for a fact.

❑b. I've always believed that what you don't know can't hurt you.

❑c. No child should be left behind, whether you know they are yours or not—unless you're taking a long trip in a small car.

❑d. No one should live with the fear that someday (especially during a press conference) someone will yell out, "Hey Pops," and really mean it.

GO ON TO THE NEXT PAGE

51. Which of the following choices would best articulate your image as the parent of the world?

- ❑**a.** Being a father/mother figure to the world can be quite exhausting at times, which is why I am entitled to a nice vacation and the use of luxury transportation.
- ❑**b.** Trying to be a role model to the world can take the best out of anyone. Or the worst, depending on my popular-opinion poll at the time.
- ❑**c.** I try to get the world to relate to all the difficulties of parenting, but it's hard to understand "dada" in so many dialects and foreign tongues.

52. Did your parents like you?________________

53. Did your parents ever tell you that you were an accident?________________________________

54. Your parents compared your birth to:

- ❑**a.** A baseball-going-through-the-kitchen-window type of accident.
- ❑**b.** A traffic accident.
- ❑**c.** A large building collapse.
- ❑**d.** A global-warming mishap.

55. How would you explain your relationship with your parents?

❑**a.** My parents did the best they could to raise me; it was just a piss-poor job.

❑**b.** My father always advised me to live within my means. After growing up as part of one of the richest families in America, do you really expect me to change?

❑**c.** My mother taught me never to hesitate when asked to do something. She told me to just start doing it, even if I don't understand what the hell they want me to do.

❑**d.** Of course, I have secret desires. At times, I wish for just one more nursing session with my mother. Doesn't everyone?

56. Which of the following is an example of a free market?

❑**a.** A car company moves its factories to Mexico.

❑**b.** A toy company outsources to a Chinese subcontractor.

❑**c.** A major bank incorporates in Bermuda to avoid taxes.

❑**d.** Americans purchase HP printers made in Mexico and shirts made in Bangladesh.

GO ON TO THE NEXT PAGE

❑**e.** Americans can purchase drugs from Canadian pharmacies.

❑**f.** You speak to someone in India when you need computer help.

FACTOID: Convicted felons receive Social Security when they reach retirement age. If they are stabbed, beaten, or injured while in prison, they receive workman's compensation. Most states prohibit them from voting, however, if they are twice-convicted felons; and some states require them to vote twice, with a vote cast for each party.

CHECK YOUR WORK AND MAKE SURE YOU DIDN'T MAKE A FOOL OF YOURSELF.

TAKE A DEEP BREATH AND CONTINUE ON TO THE NEXT CHAPTER.

WHO'S GOT THE BIG BUCKS AND WILL THEY LIVE TO SPEND IT?

CHAPTER THREE

WHAT DOES THE public need to know about your personal wealth? Here are a few items that, if unanswered, we think have the potential to become issues during an ugly campaign. (Though, there really are no pretty campaigns. It's not that people don't want to be nice to one another, but once the pressure is on, they can't seem to get beyond name-calling, accusations, and pictures of their opponents in silly hats.) Sorry, we digress again.

The following section will examine your financial status, something that is extremely important to your constituents. Discussing money is always tricky, especially if you are the POTUS. Americans want a leader who'll be able to handle the country's finances, yet the public may also become jealous of your insanely full bank accounts. Please answer the questions honestly, but if you can cleverly fudge it—and get away with it—then by all means, do so.

Financial disclosures: Please answer with yes, no, or I wish to assert my Fifth Amendment privilege.

57. Do you have a bank account?________________

58. Is it in a foreign country?________________

59. If a wiretap were placed on your phone because you make numerous calls to other countries, would you be able offer an explanation for these calls without getting arrested?________

60. Do you have foreign domestic household help?_____

61. Do you pay taxes for your domestic help?_________

62. Does your foreign help pay domestic taxes?________

63. Besides your domestic help, do you have any foreign investments?______________________________

NOTE

You may not know this, but if you were appointed to an office that required a Senate confirmation, you would have to prove that you've always been an upstanding, responsible, tax-paying citizen—meaning, yes, all your taxes are in order, even

those for domestic help. (Unless you had enough cash around to never leave a trail and were willing to do away with any loved ones who could potentially snitch on you). However, if you are running for President, you'll never be asked this question, because your campaign staff will assume you'd never be so dumb as to not cover your tracks (and besides, they are most likely afraid of you). Unless you feel guilty about your taxes, please continue.

64. When you become President, would you willingly give up your foreign help or would you make them interns?____

65. Would you give up any foreign help or investments that could be considered controversial?________________

66. How about those totally sleazy investments that no one could possibly know about—unless there's a secret surveillance camera in your home, at your office, or hidden in the garage behind your extensive porn collection?________

67. Can you account for every penny you have ever made? Do you have a paper trail that leads to a now defunct, criminally investigated accounting firm? (You know which firm we mean.)____

POTUS
Training Exercise #4

Let's pretend for a moment that you are going on a trip. You decide to drive because despite the phenomenal gas expense, you like the convenience (it's okay to admit it, we like it too). Besides, you want to encourage oil companies to keep pumping out those profits—it's good for the economy, if not the people. Anyways, the good news is that you don't have to stop at a burger joint for lunch because your mother/spouse/loved one made a sandwich for your trip. You get in your car and put your sandwich right next to your cell phone. You turn on the motor, find your favorite station on the radio, and begin to drive. It's a lovely night. The moonshine reflects brightly off your golden vehicle. (It's our make-believe story so we get to pick the colors.) The radio is blasting and you are "rocking out to the music." You wish you had brought along the ballroom shoes.

After traveling for about half an hour, you're starving. The sandwich, chips, and a drink are right there for the taking. (Well, of course there are chips and a drink. Who just packs a sandwich?) You open the sandwich, chips, and the drink with one hand. The other remains on the wheel.

The sandwich tastes wonderful and you begin to move (and chew) to the rhythm of the music that is playing. Then, your cell phone rings, startling you. You feel compelled to answer the phone, even though you are choking a bit on your sandwich. You try to take a drink to stop choking but it spills on your lap. You grab for the napkins (yes, of course there are napkins, who packs all that food without a napkin?) and drop the sandwich, which (of course) falls to the floor. You grab for the cell and the car begins to swerve. You hit the median and flip over. The car explodes and you are trapped inside.

(Sorry to disappoint you. We know that for a minute there, you thought this would be a nice imaginary story.) Now answer question 68:

GO ON TO THE NEXT PAGE

68. What are you more concerned about? The health effects of:

- ❑ **a.** Talking on your cell phone while driving.
- ❑ **b.** Eating a sandwich while driving.
- ❑ **c.** Dancing in the dark while driving.
- ❑ **d.** The employees vs. the management at Wal-Mart.

FACTOID: The President of the United States does not necessarily have to lie in state in the Capitol Rotunda. A President can choose the site for this honor. Or the President might elect not to lie in state at all. A 1960s-generation President could go on a road trip with the Rolling Stones.

Speaking of that great American corporation, the following story illustrates just what makes Wal-Mart such a great company. (Did you think we included that answer just to throw you off? We needed a way to segue into this Wal-Mart story. Smart, aren't we?)

"Listen, you don't have to spend that kind of money," Mike replies. "There's a diagnostic computer down at Wal-Mart. Just give it a urine sample and it'll tell you what's wrong and what to do about it. It takes ten seconds and costs ten dollars, which is lot easier and cheaper than seeing a doctor."

This seems like a good idea to Joe, who deposits a urine sample in a small jar and takes it to Wal-Mart. He pays his ten dollars. The computer lights up and asks for the urine sample, which he pours into the slot. Ten seconds later, the computer ejects a printout:

"You have tennis elbow. Soak your arm in warm water and avoid heavy activity. It will improve in two weeks. Thank you for shopping @ Wal-Mart."

That evening while thinking how amazing this new technology was, Joe began to wonder if he could fool the computer. He mixes some tap water, a stool sample from his dog, urine samples from his wife and daughter, and a sperm sample, for good measure. He hurries back to Wal-Mart, eager to check the results. He pays ten dollars, pours in his concoction, and awaits the results.

GO ON TO THE NEXT PAGE

> The computer prints the following:
>
> 1. Your tap water is too hard Get a water softener (aisle 9).
> 2. Your dog has ringworm. Bathe him with antifungal shampoo (aisle 7).
> 3. Your daughter has a cocaine habit. Get her into rehab.
> 4. Your wife is pregnant. Twins. They arent yours. Get a lawyer.
> 5. If you dont stop playing with yourself, your elbow will never get better!
>
> Thank you for shopping @ Wal-Mart.

At this point, you may be wondering where we're going with this story. The answer is nowhere; we just like that story a lot. And we like Wal-Mart a lot too.

✎ **69.** The American economy is dependent on the success of companies like Wal-Mart. What would you advise Wal-Mart do to get through this constant haranguing by the media as well as demonstrate that they really are a "God Bless America" company?

- ❑**a.** Cave in to the politicians who insist they give healthy portions of their profits to underwrite health-care plans for employees.
- ❑**b.** Fight back. Jack up prices, cut the number of employees, and insist every employee fill out a personal medical history. Then cut all medical

benefits to everyone who is obese (unless they attend and show improvement in a Weight Watchers program), everyone who smokes (unless they attend and show improvement in a quit-smoking program), and everyone else who doesn't eat at least three green vegetables a day.

❑**c.** Move on. Lower prices for blue-collar family photos. (Yes, of course they have to wear blue collars—it's part of the message). And make sure that there is always a patriotic or holiday backdrop used for background. At the same time, raise prices on photos of single, rich looking, thin, white people who request any Caribbean-looking backdrop. It sends a message about the kind of customer the Wal-Martian appreciates.

Unfortunately, Wal-Mart is always a target for the media despite the fact that it's a place a lot of "real" people frequent. Let's see what you've learned from visiting other places that "real" people frequent.

70. Let's say you find yourself at a Dunkin' Donuts. (No, you can't go to Starbucks; we're looking for real people, remember?) Look at the list below and decide which of these statements are true.

❑**a.** Fat people always start to eat at the counter while they are still paying for their donuts.

GO ON TO THE NEXT PAGE

- ❑**b.** Men who carry their money in their wallets are probably gay.
- ❑**c.** Men who have a hard time picking out an assorted dozen of donuts are usually unsuccessful.
- ❑**d.** Men who ask for a dozen plain donuts are generally successful.
- ❑**e.** Men who ask for fourteen donuts and eat the extra two on the way back to the office are generally embezzlers.
- ❑**f.** Men who eat a dozen donuts and only take two back to the office are probably Republicans.
- ❑**g.** Men who order a dozen donuts and give half of them away to a panhandler are probably Democrats.
- ❑**h.** Fat women who eat their donuts right out of the bag always wipe their fingers on their butts as if to say, "That's where it's going anyway."
- ❑**i.** Skinny people who order a dozen donuts and one small plain coffee will generally drop the bag in the parking lot, put them back into the bag without wiping them off, and proceed back to the office, where their colleagues will enjoy them as a treat.
- ❑**j.** Young people usually order a single jelly donut, which they'll probably share in their car.
- ❑**k.** People who count out the exact change for their orders should be hit from behind and mugged.
- ❑**l.** People who carry different denominations of bills in different pockets are absolutely paranoid.

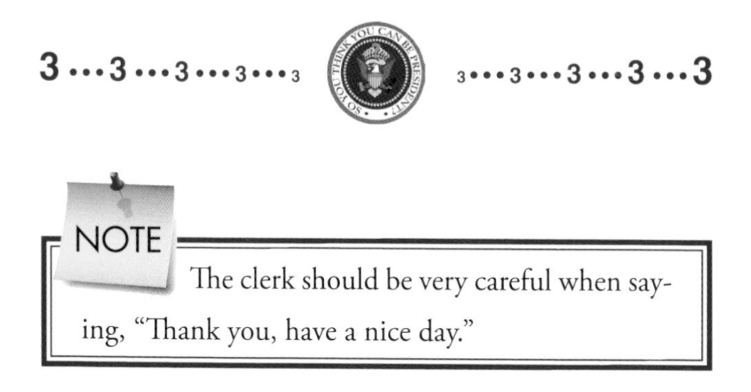

NOTE

The clerk should be very careful when saying, "Thank you, have a nice day."

CHECK YOUR WORK AND MAKE SURE YOU DIDN'T MAKE A FOOL OF YOURSELF.

TAKE A DEEP BREATH AND CONTINUE ON TO THE NEXT CHAPTER.

SELECTING SENIOR OFFICIALS AND THE CABINET

(Or, What Is an Intern Really Supposed to Do?)

CHAPTER FOUR

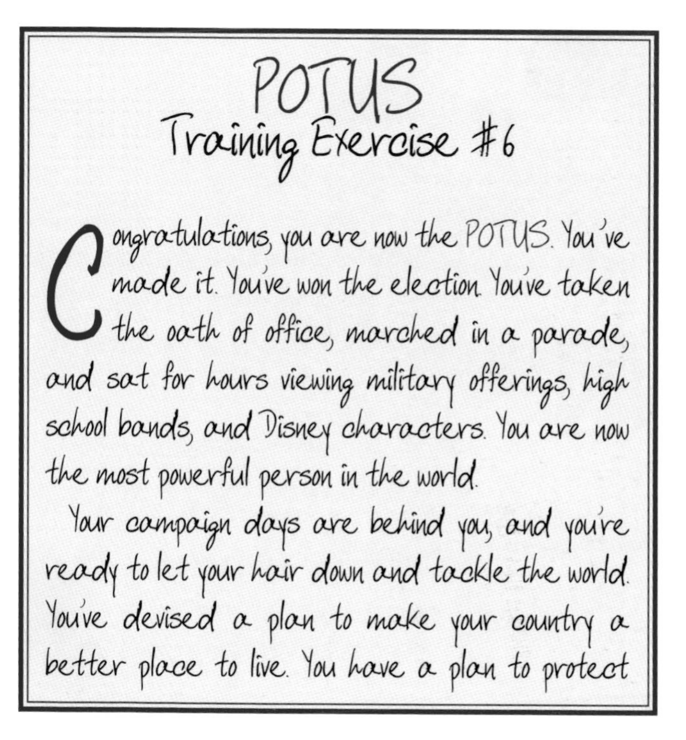

POTUS
Training Exercise #6

Congratulations, you are now the POTUS. You've made it. You've won the election. You've taken the oath of office, marched in a parade, and sat for hours viewing military offerings, high school bands, and Disney characters. You are now the most powerful person in the world.

Your campaign days are behind you, and you're ready to let your hair down and tackle the world. You've devised a plan to make your country a better place to live. You have a plan to protect

them, solace them in time of need, and guide the country to its rightful place in the world. You know all the words to "God Bless America," "The National Anthem," and "Proud to Be an American." And like each of your predecessors, you've gathered advice from a million different experts.

NOTE

Not only does it look better to talk to experts, it's also easier to have people in place to blame when things go wrong. You have everything at your disposal to make your term a great one.

NOT SO FAST. The American people may have elected you as their President, but it's only the beginning. The public will be watching you like an owl (owls can see at night), noting every move you take and every change you make. This is a critical time for a new President because Americans are still trying to gauge your ability to run this country. Even your most trivial decisions will be weighed and measured against you.

This next section will test how you will respond to the trivial—yet still important—details that you, as the Presi-

dent, will have to decide upon. And what better time to decide upon the trivial than at the beginning, seeing as how you have no clue what you are doing yet. Some questions may seem extremely silly to you, but we assure you, America will be on its toes, awaiting your answers.

And you thought the campaign was difficult.

71. As the President of the United States, you must present yourself as being strictly in line with the moral and ethical codes of humanity. Yet, as much as you preach that standard of behavior to all of your subordinates, you may forget that it also applies to you as well. Below are some examples of the misuse of Presidential power. Select one or more that you'd like to see corrected.

❑ **a.** You would like proper credit given to the people who help to produce Presidential public events. (For example, the "Chairman of the Board," Mr. Frank Sinatra, always recognized Paul Anka for writing the song "My Way." It's just a nice touch to do so.) Every televised Presidential appearance should run credits for the speechwriter, wardrobe, hair, makeup and audio enhancement, et cetera. The key phrase here is "giving credit where credit is due."

❑ **b.** People who are constantly in the public eye always recognize the sponsors who've helped them along the way. Tiger Woods, Dale Earnhardt Jr., Martha Stewart, and Bill Gates are all examples of people

GO ON TO THE NEXT PAGE

who display some emblem or insignia representing those who support them. Shouldn't the President do so as well? Would you, as President, have a jackass or an elephant embroidered on all your jackets, hats, and outerwear? Or have the logos from your major campaign contributors displayed in the Oval Office, or on your limousine and Air Force One?

❑ **c.** Correct the image of being just another "talking head" and become a "real" American. Stop wearing those covert listening devices that give you instructions on how to answer a question during a press briefing or debate. Wouldn't it make more sense to be more human and less animated? For instance, when asked a question, wouldn't it be refreshing to give an answer like, "Hell, Geraldo, you know I have no idea what you're talking about. Next."

72. What about staffing the government? Where do you start? Put your thinking cap on and answer yes or no to the following questions.

> NOTE
>
> Don't dismiss any of these options without thinking about both the positive and negative aspects of the hire. We've tried to point you in the right direction with a few helpful hints.

- ❑ **a.** Would you hire someone who has worked in a former Administration? (They may know something about how the government works.)
- ❑ **b.** Would you hire people who have belonged to a cult? (They're probably loyal to a fault and good at following directions.)
- ❑ **c.** Would you hire someone who insists on wearing Groucho glasses and a mustache to work? (This person has most likely worked undercover or on a 1950s game show. Either way, they'll understand the importance of covert activity.)
- ❑ **d.** Would you hire someone who has won a game show? You'll never have to explain how important it is to win a contest with this person. (This may be useful during your next campaign.)

> **NOTE**
>
> During a Presidential reelection campaign, anyone without a title, and who will not be missed or investigated by the press, "works on the campaign."

73. Some people think that the official Presidential anthem, "Hail to the Chief," is old and that the President should have a new, contemporary tune. As some say, "The times they are a-changin'." As you might've guessed, we

GO ON TO THE NEXT PAGE

want you to put your thinking cap on and decide which of the following songs you would choose to celebrate your celebrity.

- ❑ **a.** "We Are Family."
- ❑ **b.** "Forever in Blue Jeans."
- ❑ **c.** "The Man Who Shot Liberty Valance."
- ❑ **d.** "A Hard Day's Night."

74. In addition to deciding which music is played, who would you like to have sing the song and where should they be?

- ❑ **a.** Master at Arms of the Senate prior to the State of the Union, on the front steps of the Capitol.
- ❑ **b.** Senators, Representatives, and departmental employees, at the White House during a Presidential arrival, preferably while the helicopter is whirring.
- ❑ **c.** Cabinet appointees who are doing a "follow the bouncing ball" sing along in the East Room during a diplomatic dinner.

75. Each President recites the Oath of Office, in accordance with Article II, Section I, of the US Constitution. You cannot be the President unless you put your hand on a Bible and say:

"I do solemnly swear (or affirm) that I will faithfully execute the office of President of the United States, and will to the best

of my ability, preserve, protect, and defend the Constitution of the United States."

If you could amend the Constitution and change this oath to something a bit more contemporary, which of the following would you choose?

❑**a.** Bodily oath: I hereby swear in blood and other precious bodily fluids that I will perform, without hesitation, any and all desires of the POTUS. And if I cannot do so, for some physiological or psychological reason, I'll find someone who will.

❑**b.** Oath of secrecy: I swear that I will not divulge, ever, who I am or what my purpose in life is. This oath will extend not only to my family and parents but to myself as well.

❑**c.** Hypocritical oath: (No, we didn't make a spelling error, this is about the Presidency—not medicine.) I announce unto the gods: Charlatan, Pretender, and Fraud, that I will endeavor to follow in their light. I swear that no matter what I say or do, I will believe I am right and will try my best to convince others of my sincerity, no matter how many times I'm impeached.

76. Presidents don't usually apologize for any mistakes they've made. (This is practically a Presidential tradition.) Instead, they insist that the more menial task-doers (and we "meanial" this in the nicest possible way) make amends

GO ON TO THE NEXT PAGE

for both their mistakes and the President's. Before you hire anyone for a senior job, they need to know how you want them to deal with screw-ups. Which of the following do you prefer as a technique for handling blunders?

❑**a.** Deny, deny, deny. The more you repeat that there was no mistake, the more likely a bigger news story will come along and people will forget your mistake.

❑**b.** Lie, lie, lie. If the powers that be can come up with a really big, believable whopper, you might as well capitalize on it. Besides, isn't it better for the public to believe their elected leader is infallible?

❑**c.** Cry, cry, cry. Use the old sympathy trick. Make the public feel that you made a boo-boo but only because you thought you were doing the right or ignoble (or did we mean noble . . .) thing for them.

❑**d.** Die, die, die. Find someone who is just expendable enough to not be missed when you hang them out to dry. Or even better, when you shoot them blindfolded at dawn on the front lawn of the White House.

77. On the other hand, do you think you should change this tradition and apologize for the things you have done that were naughty, ridiculous, illegal, or unethical? If your answer is no, do you think you should be counseled by:

❑ **a.** The God Squad (Yes, there really is a God Squad).

❑ **b.** A deaf and mute, but understanding, psychiatrist.

❑ **c.** The best lobbying and PR firm you can find.

78. If your answer is yes, you must instruct the "menials" on how to respond to questions from both the media and the public. Answer the following questions with a yes or no, depending on whether the question is similar to your own thinking or whoever does your thinking for you. (And no lengthy responses, please.)

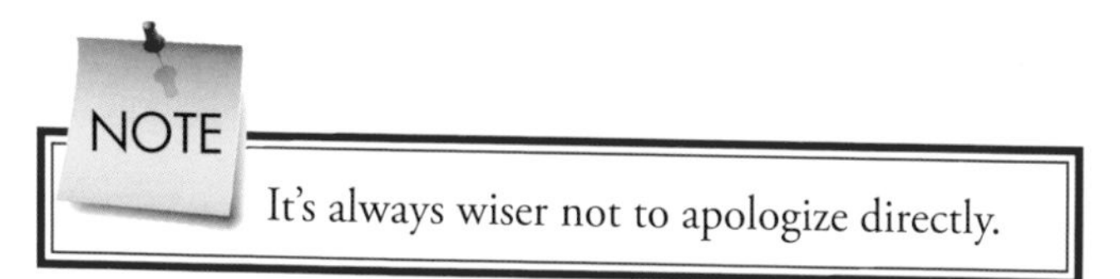

It's always wiser not to apologize directly.

❑ **a.** When discussing other people's tragedies, is making the sign of the cross really an acceptable way to apologize?

❑ **b.** Is merely saying you're doing the best you can enough to clear you of any guilt?

❑ **c.** All of us in the room know you're sorry. Hell, the whole country knows you're sorry. The question we're all wondering is, are you sorry for destroying some sick chickens contaminated with bird flu or for the mess it made?

GO ON TO THE NEXT PAGE

- ❑ **d.** You are frequently apologizing to our country for the ineptness of your staff and cabinet members; don't you think firing them would be more in line?
- ❑ **e.** Mr. President, do you realize that when you say, "I can feel what you're feeling," that there is no way for that to be true unless you have your hand in my pocket?
- ❑ **f.** Without looking, are there more vowels than consonants in the word apologize?
- ❑ **g.** Isn't being on your knees with outstretched arms, while begging for forgiveness, a bit much?

FACTOID: No President has ever received a Grammy or an Oscar for best actor in a drama series. However, the Screen Actors Guild has handed out awards to several Presidents for Best Stand-Up Comedian in a Drama Series.

The POTUS's first order of business is to figure out what you really know about being President and all that entails—the government, its agencies, et cetera. Your second order of business? Finding a trustworthy, intelligent, and crafty staff—with just a little bit of shadiness—who can fill you in on everything you don't know. (You don't expect your staff to be squeaky clean, do you? Keep in mind, these are the folk who'll be saving your behind!)

This part of the test is meant to give the electorate an idea of how much you already know and, based on that, how much you will have to learn. (Try to remain calm.) You may think you're smart, but are you knowledgeable of everything about which the POTUS needs to be knowledgeable? (See, you're confused already.) This section will also address your ability to surround yourself with the "right" people. Are your human resources skills in good order? We hope so!

POTUS Training Exercise #7

Now that you've surrounded yourself with all the right people, it's time to get down to business. You call your coaches in for a meeting to outline what they'll need to do to accomplish all your goals. Before the meeting starts, your newly appointed Chief of Staff raises a hand and says, "Mr. President, I have some interesting facts that I'd like to present before we hear your thoughts."

This is your first meeting and because you want

GO ON TO THE NEXT PAGE

to appear magnanimous, you agree, figuring that it looks generous to allow someone else to be the first to speak. Since you're new to this game, you can also use the additional time to figure out what to say.

The Chief of Staff begins by saying, "Mr. President, all the people in this room are here for one reason and that is to follow your orders and help you to define your place in history."

Everyone in the room stands and applauds. You start to feel Presidential. But then the Chief of Staff continues, "Mr. President, you've won this election by fifty-one percent of the vote and all those constituents are one hundred percent behind you. But this means that forty-nine percent of Americans will probably remain against you."

The room is quiet and the smiles begin to disappear. You don't say anything because you have no idea why the Chief of Staff has brought this up. You look at him and say the only thing that comes to mind, "So?"

"Mr. President, you're like a football team owner who only has half of a team. You need to decide whether we're going to have an offensive team or a defensive team. The problem is that no matter which you choose, you'll never be able to win any game you play."

You have no idea what the hell he's talking about and moreover, you hate confusing football analogies. You want to shout, "Sit down and shut up!" Instead, you remain calm and reply, "So, what can we do, Chief of Staff?"

79. "Well, Mr. President, the choice is yours. Here are the options":

- ❑**a.** Try to make friends in Congress and see what you can accomplish working alongside all the branches of government.
- ❑**b.** Figure out how to have four years of fun and let someone else worry about the clean up.
- ❑**c.** Suggest having caviar and champagne daily and revel in the staff's exclamations, like, "You da man, boss."

GO ON TO THE NEXT PAGE

Extra credit if you came up with:

❑**d.** Call the Secret Service and ask them to remove a football-analogy-loving wacko from the senior staff meeting.

80. How many government jobs are politically appointed? Too hard? Okay, move on, but you're missing a great opportunity to show your knowledge here.______________

81. How many interns can you have at your disposal? Too dangerous to answer without counsel? We understand. Okay, skip to the next question.____________________

82. What qualifications should the people you want to appoint have in order to be considered for a position? For example, do you believe that everyone from your home state is qualified to do something? Do you intend to keep finding and creating positions until everyone in your home state is employed?______________________________

83. You were right to "pshaw" the last question. But do you believe that more than half of all political appointees should be from your home state?__________________

84. Do you think that as part of their employment test they should be able to sing the state song? If yes, please sing the chorus and be sure to finish by acknowledging the state

flower. Too difficult? Okay, then, move right along to the names of your best friends in high school.___________

85. If your best friends are very rich, in which agency will you put their children?_______________________

86. Would you create new agencies if your best friends' children didn't like your choice of agencies?__________

87. If you do decide to create new agencies, what would they be? Choose from the following.

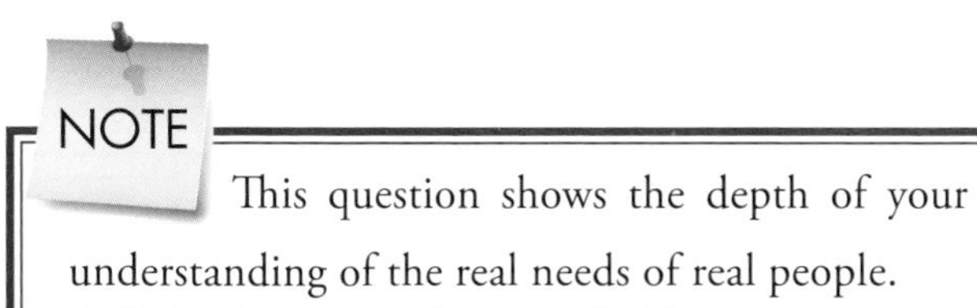

- ❑**a.** Agency for International Understanding.
- ❑**b.** Agency for Multicultural Understanding.
- ❑**c.** Agency for Researching Useless Information.

88. If you felt that International or Multicultural Understanding were very important and you selected one of those answers, goodie for you. Now, please explain, briefly, what in the world an agency that wants to "understand" anything would do. (If you selected c., then it's obvious you understand the critical need to find unimportant jobs for

GO ON TO THE NEXT PAGE

mediocre people. It's astounding how many people overlook this.)____

____

____

89. In addition to a statement of personal/financial history for all potential Cabinet applicants, do you agree that they should also include an addendum describing what they intend to do after government service? We've provided some questions for that addendum below. Please answer (yes or no) whether or not these questions should be included.

- ❑**a.** After your tenure in the White House, will you consider lobbying as a second career? On balance, isn't payback an important part of empire building?
- ❑**b.** Will you publish your memoirs, highlighting how your President made profound and positive effects on the country? In particular, pointing out that the only reason the President took such long vacations was to cover up the time he needed to rewrite the Bill of Rights and the Constitution.
- ❑**c.** Will you allow a self-destructive chip to be inserted in somewhere in your body that could be used (as a fail-safe device) to prevent you from writing a tell-all book in case you become a born again Christian?
- ❑**d.** Can you write a 2,500-word essay on the similarities between unions and Communism?

❑ **e.** How about an essay that especially targets the mandatory minimum wage act? Do you agree employees should only be paid for what they're worth?

90. Do you believe the Surgeon General will give you free medical advice?______________________________

If you've answered "yes," you may be surprised to learn that the Surgeon General is not a surgeon, nor is he a general. That wasn't necessarily a trick question, but it goes to show that you really need to do some reading before you make any other appointments.

These were difficult, thought-provoking questions. Try to get a grip and go on.

POTUS
Training Exercise #8

Let's assume that the previous President was from the other party. Given this, it's likely that the current politically appointed personnel are not part of your party. You may not believe us, but this is actually good news because

GO ON TO THE NEXT PAGE

it's always easier to replace the enemy than to drag your friends kicking and screaming from large, easily seen public office buildings.

Your first decision is to figure out who you should hire to replace these enemies in your current staff. Before you begin firing and hiring, here's a bit of information that may make hiring good people for government jobs even more difficult: government salaries are dictated by the federal-salary schedules. This means that you're not going to be able to buy great talent. Instead, you'll have to be very creative with your appeals and promises for the future, because it'll be difficult to find someone (let alone a smart someone) who is willing to take tremendous pay cuts just for the glory of being a Presidential appointee.

Just to give you some sense of what you are dealing with, a GS 15, the highest government-service employee, has a starting salary of $88,000 before taxes. A server in the world famous Sloppy Joe's Bar in Key West, Florida, earns more than that and most of it is nontaxable. Or how about this

example: a Level I Senior Executive has a starting salary of $175,000, which is peanuts compared to a plumber in the Hamptons, who makes more than $300,000 annually. Sure, this seems odd, but this is how the government—your government now—works.

The real question you have to ask yourself is, "When I hire this person, can I trust them with a government credit card?"

91. Which of the following positions do you think the average campaign worker might be qualified to do (and find interesting too) in your administration?

- ❑**a.** Part-time security guard.
- ❑**b.** Performing flight attendant duties when you fly on Air Force One.
- ❑**c.** Babysitting for visiting foreign dignitaries who have children.
- ❑**d.** Bartender for official functions. (Of course they can display a tip jar!)

92. Once you've hired a press secretary you can make all kinds of announcements. (That's why you have a press secretary—so you can deny that you ever said anything.)

When hiring the press secretary, which of the following traits would you look for?

GO ON TO THE NEXT PAGE

❑**a.** In addition to English, he can also speak in tongues.

❑**b.** A speech defect to make it easier to say there was a misunderstanding. If possible, select someone with a heavy stutter. It will reduce the number of questions asked and reporters may even feel a sense of sympathy or embarrassment. (Wouldn't that be a first?) This in turn will encourage less complicated questions.

❑**c.** Someone who is short. Hiring a very short person will eliminate the tension of having to look into the eyes of anyone asking questions. If that's not possible, would you agree to build a very high lectern so only the forehead can be seen?

93. To ensure our safety and health, food handlers in this country are required to wash their hands every time they use the bathroom, wear either a hairnet or some other form of head cover, and use rubber gloves. Which of the following precautions would you adopt to effectively ensure you are safe from any annoying press inquiries? (You were thinking this question belonged with health issues, didn't you? We told you there would be tricks.)

❑**a.** Prior to a press conference, duct-tape your press secretary's arms around his waist so he can't point to the next questioner.

❑b. Make sure your press secretary has a healthy dose of nighttime cough medicine before any daytime press meeting, making him drowsy and his speech slurred. This way, the meeting will pass quickly with yawns, rubbing of eyes, and several calls of "would you repeat that question, please?"

❑c. Hire a voice coach for the press secretary and insist that all answers be sung instead of spoken. Provide a long list of lyrics that can be memorized and will fit any occasion. Among those we would suggest:

"Let's Hang on to What We Got"
"Leaving on a Jet Plane"
"Long Distance Information, Please Give Me the Vice-President"
"The Name Game"
"Lonely Teardrops"
"I Heard It Through the Grapevine"
"Who Do You Love . . . Who Do You Love?"
"Don't Make Me Over"

❑d. Create a sing-along to end the press briefing on a light and bubbly note. The lyrics to "We Are Family" or "That's What Friends Are For" could be projected on a large screen and participants can follow the bouncing Presidential seal.

94. You've decided to take on the media by suggesting new titles for their shows. If you were going to appear on a

GO ON TO THE NEXT PAGE

popular news show, which of the following would you find most desirable?

- ❑**a.** *Anderson Cooper: 180 Degrees.* (Only half is true and the viewer has to figure out which half.)
- ❑**b.** *The Saturation Room with Wolf Blitzer.* (If he repeats a story more than six times, the viewer can email in and win earplugs or a Blitzer Condom.)
- ❑**c.** *Chris Matthews: Hardballs.* (He appears to be in so much pain that he can't complete a sentence and interrupts his guests just to end the show as soon as possible.)
- ❑**d.** *Bill O'Reilly's The Spinout Zone.* (Just when it gets interesting, his guests walk off the show and the picture goes black.)

95. Who do you absolutely have to make sure gets a job?

- ❑**a.** Campaign workers.
- ❑**b.** Fundraisers.
- ❑**c.** Experts. (But only the ones who actually know something about something.)

96. Why is it necessary to have pictures of interns before they get hired?

- ❑**a.** Unattractive interns interfere with the image of the beautiful America that you're trying to create.

❑ **b.** You need to set some form of standards for your administration and good grooming is high on the list.

❑ **c.** Your senior staff is more likely to work late if they have desirable companionship.

97. If you had to replace the head of the Federal Reserve, which of the following would you consider?

❑ **a.** Pardoning a convicted CEO who defrauded his corporation out of billions. You can feel confident that he definitely has talent in the financial world.

❑ **b.** Making the Federal Reserve a for-profit business and then charging for consulting.

❑ **c.** Initiating a merger between the World Bank, Federal Reserve, and organized gambling to ensure an adequate cash flow at all times.

NOTE

Consider that with the addition of an Organized Gambling department, loans would be paid without having to acknowledge or forgive them.

98. As President, would you allow a person without credentials or experience to be placed in a critical job where people's lives depended on their decision-making?______

GO ON TO THE NEXT PAGE

FACTOID: The federal government is usually so far in debt that they can't even get a loan from the SBA.

99. Would you remove an incompetent appointee from the job?__________________________________

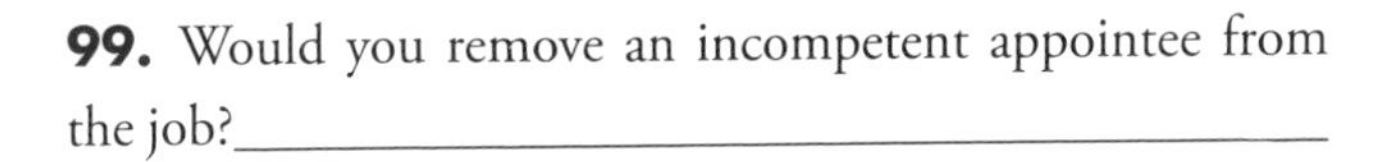

100. If potential appointees say that they can't start their job until they have finished a honeymoon, sent their child to college, or straightened up their finances, would you:

- ❑**a.** Think about whether or not these people are serious about the work.
- ❑**b.** Look at their work history.
- ❑**c.** Appoint a deputy who has been involved with the work for more than six months.
- ❑**d.** Thank them for working on your campaign.

101. Will your appointees know how to play (and win) the blame game? Which of the following do you think is most important?

- ❑**a.** The ability to be belligerent and arrogant when they are called on by Congress to testify about a big screwup.
- ❑**b.** How they will look in handcuffs after being indicted.

❑c. That they are willing to lay the blame on a trusted friend or relative.

❑d. That their job is important enough to insure a lucrative lobbying job after they leave government (whether forcibly or amicably).

102. In times of trouble and bad publicity, many people on your staff will want to jump ship before they take a hit. Which of the following solutions do you think would be the most effective way to keep them on staff?

❑a. Promise that if they are ever found guilty of anything, you'll grant them a pardon.

❑b. Promise a huge pension plan if they stay with you for ten years. (You are golden if they believe this, because they probably don't realize that you're limited to serving only eight years.)

❑c. Promise that you'll make sure they get to the head of the line for a FEMA house trailer. (Just in case their homes are destroyed by disaster. You never know.)

❑d. Promise that they'll be allowed to peruse the Patriot Act personal files to find interesting items about their friends that they can use to their advantage.

NOTE

When making these offers, always be sure to say, "I would never lie to you or the American people."

GO ON TO THE NEXT PAGE

103. Speaking of troubled times, let's say that you encounter some problems during the course of your administration. This is bound to happen because it's human nature (not yours, necessarily) not to strive for perfection if you're working for a company you don't own. And, try as you might to give away large chunks of the government, the staff will never believe it's theirs to sell. Unfortunately, this means that people will make mistakes and the public will blame you. So how do you avoid having a Presidential pardon hanging over your head like Richard Nixon? Or being arrested and fined $20 for exceeding the Washington speed limit for a horse like Ulysses S. Grant? Or being nicknamed "Uncle Jumbo" like President Grover Cleveland? Or worst of all, being offered a contract to pitch for the Cincinnati Reds like William H. Taft? In short, how would you preserve your legacy?

❑**a.** Instead of having what might be considered a personal and damaging conversation in the Oval Office, where you know it will be taped, get off the old duffer and walk down the hall to the East Wing, go to the men's room, and lock the door.

❑**b.** Create a videotape of every move you ever made while in office. Then, when you retire, have all the bad stuff edited out so you can produce your own infomercial, reaffirming how wonderful all those years were. Remember to distribute the

DVDs free of charge—people will take anything free from TV.

❑**c.** Whenever you appoint anyone to a position of power, make them sign a contract agreeing that when they get lucrative lobbying jobs, media positions, or big corporate jobs, they will spend at least 150 hours a week speaking about your accomplishments in office.

104. Since we're still on the subject of problems, what's more problematic than nominating a Supreme Court Justice? And what makes it such a difficult job? Quite simply, it's the word "supreme." If you look in the *Oxford American Dictionary,* "supreme" is defined as: highest in importance, intensity, and quality. If, however, you look at the people who do or have occupied the spaces, these adjectives do not always apply. This shouldn't be your concern. Your job is to find someone who is truly supreme and get him or her confirmed. Confirmation is always cumbersome because the Senate Judiciary Committee usually votes along party lines. If your party is not in power, you are in deep doo-doo. Which of the following steps would you take to speed up the process?

❑**a.** Instead of a bipartisan committee serving all the time, have the Senators from the same party serve every other month.

❑**b.** Have the nominee flip a coin. Heads they are confirmed, tails they pack their bags and go back to chasing ambulances.

❑**c.** The nominees should never testify. Instead, have their mother, spouse, or household help (you know, the people who know the truth about the nominees' abilities) answer the pertinent questions about issues of national importance.

105. Before you go to the trouble of finding a supreme lawyer (which for the most part is an oxymoron—with the definition of oxymoron being someone who is eight times more moronic than most people), know that the Constitution does not establish any qualifications for the Justices of the Supreme Court. The person you select doesn't even have to be a citizen or old enough to vote. This certainly opens up the field from which to choose a "supremist." From the list below, choose the person who is the most similar to the type of Justice you would want during your Administration. (You'll notice that the list is composed of only celebrity types. This was intentional. Given the long process for confirmation, we felt that a person who was already in the public eye would fare far better.)

❑**a.** If you have ever watched *Law & Order* (or any of the spin-offs, *Law & Order: Special Victims Unit*, *Law & Order: Criminal Intent*, or the ill-

fated *Law & Order: Trial by Jury*), you know the name Dick Wolfe. If you haven't watched a single episode, you are out of touch with people and have no business making a choice for a local dogcatcher, let alone a Supreme Court Justice. Dick Wolfe is the creator and executive producer of these hit shows. Just from the names of his shows, surely it's obvious that he understands the full range of courts' responsibilities. He's a person who could make decisions about the death penalty, civil liberties, and pausing for commercial breaks. He can't be messed with.

❑ **b.** Barbara Streisand. Who could be wiser than this maven of music? Wasn't it Babs who insightfully said that people who know people are the luckiest people in the world? (Okay, you got us. She sang it. It still came out of her mouth.)

❑ **c.** Arnold Schwarzenegger has proven to be both a hero and a man of action. No one would argue that he is supreme. Just look at what he's done since 1982 (and the types of roles he's played): *The Terminator*, *Terminator 2: Judgment Day*, *True Lies*, *Total Recall*, *Batman and Robin*, *Eraser*, *Kindergarten Cop*, *Predator*, *Last Action Hero*, *Conan the Barbarian*, *The Running Man*, *Commando*, *Red Heat*, and *Conan*

the Destroyer. Hold up. Arnold is on the wrong list. We meant for him to be on the list for Secretary of Defense.

❑ **d.** The Naked Cowboy, who has traveled all over the globe. Regardless of the weather, he's always in his underwear meeting simple, plain folk; incarcerated felons; and the crème de la crème of many different societies. He has experienced controversy, felt the pulse of the world (the reality is that he must stand close to anyone who wants a picture taken), and understands the importance of dissension and symbolic red-white-and-blue glittery costumes.

The person you appoint will have to make critical decisions about the direction of the nation. The following pre-question story allows you to see the scope of supreme decision-making.

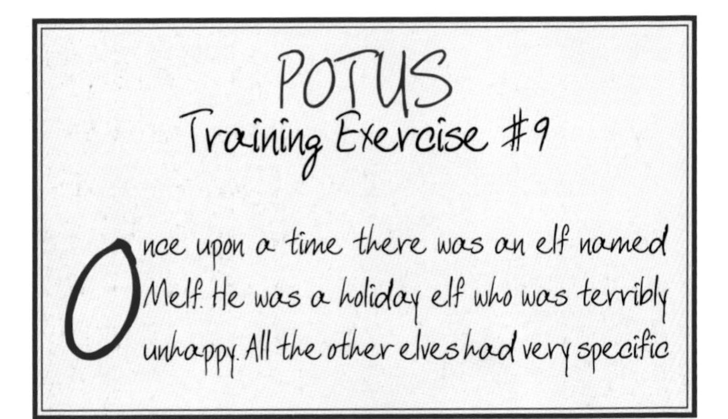

holidays, like Christmas, Hanukkah, Kwanzaa, Groundhog Day, Memorial Day, Halloween, Easter, Tu Bishvat, Saint Patrick's Day, Thanksgiving, Ramadan (which is not an inn), Baha'i, Chinese New Year, Labor Day, Vesak Day, Martin Luther King Jr.'s Birthday, Malaysia Day, Diwali (except Sabah and Sarawak), Kuala Lumpur Day, Uzbekistan Unity Day, Flag Day, May Day, Father's Day, Mother's Day, Grandparent's Day, and Ash Wednesday. All of Melf's friends knew who and what they were, based on the day they were responsible for. They spent the whole year talking about the customs, costumes, decorations, food, games, and rituals involved with their holiday. But not Melf. He had no special day to define him or even to look forward to. Since he was an unspecified holiday elf, he didn't even know if he belonged to a church or a state. He spent most of the year in therapy, trying to find his center, or as some would say, his core. Poor Melf. As the POTUS, can you help Melf?

GO ON TO THE NEXT PAGE

106. In case you hadn't guessed (because it's not our job to make this easy), this question, which deals with the issue of separation of church and state, does not fit into any of the chapters. Why do you think it doesn't fit?

- ❑ **a.** Church, synagogues, mosques, prayer mounds, and temples don't belong on a test about the Presidency.
- ❑ **b.** God doesn't have a particular state or holiday, so why waste a whole chapter on moot questions?
- ❑ **c.** Spending time on this issue is like trying to help Melf. He is only one elf. Helping Melf through a personal crisis is like trying to find the cure for a disease that only a million people might have. There's no profit in it for pharmaceutical companies, so why bother? Besides, you'll never be able to satisfy all the Melfs who come along afterwards expecting some handout.

And now a, brief word about earmarks (no, they have nothing to do with your ears):

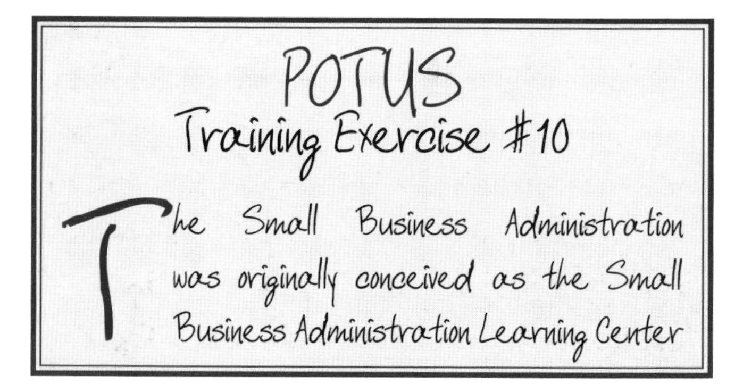

(SBALC). It was supposed to be a trade school where uneducated and illiterate individuals were given entry-level administrative courses. These support employees eventually filled vacancies that were created by the "bigger is better" or as it's more commonly called, "the more, the merrier" expansion of the federal government after the Second World War. The pay and benefits of these jobs were paltry in comparison to jobs held by nongovernmental employees. But someone had to create a bureaucracy and, unfortunately, this contributed to the large number of "common-sense challenged" applicants.

After a period of time, there were more than enough people to fill all the vacancies in the newly formed departments, agencies, and cafeterias. The problem was what to do with the SBLAC. There were too many teachers, mentors, and night maintenance personnel on the payroll to eliminate it. As a result, the SBLAC became the SBA and it served to help other small businesses with loans.

GO ON TO THE NEXT PAGE

This was the beginning of deficit spending and earmarking. In order to receive a very low-interest loan from the SBA, the borrower must have been rejected from three different lending institutions. This meant that anyone who was granted an SBA loan would probably default and the government was left with a bad debt.

The public would never have agreed to this prototype for business, so the only way for the SBA to continue was to keep this information from the public by earmarking the funds, hiding them in a complicated bill. The President can sign any bill which disguises things that might be controversial.

107. With that in mind, look at the following list of past earmarks and choose two or three that, as President, you would be sure to enhance or duplicate.

- ❑ **a.** $223 million to build a bridge to an island with fifty inhabitants.
- ❑ **b.** $115 million to construct a replica slave ship (as a form of transportation).

- ❑ **c.** $4.2 million for intermodal transportation at a zoo.
- ❑ **d.** $6 million for intermodal transportation at a bigger zoo.
- ❑ **e.** $3 million for wartime laser dental floss so the troops can clean without water or brushing.
- ❑ **f.** $2.3 million for landscaping enhancements "for aesthetic purposes" along a highway.
- ❑ **g.** $3.6 million worth of time on sanctioned Internet porn sites, to relieve military stress.
- ❑ **h.** $1.3 million for sidewalk lighting and landscaping around a small medical center.
- ❑ **i.** $4.8 million to widen a road leading to one of the Marine Corps' major training bases.
- ❑ **j.** $7 million for a new Disney ride that replicates riding in a tank in the Middle East.
- ❑ **k.** $3.3 million for a secret underground swimming pool located in Hot Springs, Arkansas.
- ❑ **l.** $1.2 million for chartering a private aircraft and a veterinarian to care for Presidential pets to accompany Air Force One.
- ❑ **m.** $1.5 million to charter a private aircraft and a veterinarian to care for Presidential pets who can't travel on Air Force One.
- ❑ **n.** $6 million for building a championship golf course on a small ranch that will be a scheduled stop on the PGA after the President leaves office.

GO ON TO THE NEXT PAGE

108. Which of the following do you think Presidents should carry in their wallet?

- ❑**a.** One health-care information card.
- ❑**b.** A Social Security card.
- ❑**c.** A driver's license.
- ❑**d.** A "donation of body parts" card.
- ❑**e.** Money.

109. Depending on your social schedule and your physical ability, you'll need to develop an appropriate Presidential hobby. Which of the following hobbies hold the most appeal for you?

- ❑**a.** Riding in cars, boats, airplanes, and trains.
- ❑**b.** Building model cars, boats, airplanes, and trains.
- ❑**c.** Windsurfing. (You're right, that's ridiculous. Move on.)
- ❑**d.** Hockey or softball. (It's unlikely that you'll be hurt by a wild softball pitch from an angry constituent, but unfortunately, we can't guarantee the same with hockey pucks.)
- ❑**e.** Knitting, sewing, or crocheting. (You can brand all the White House pets with your party's logo.)
- ❑**f.** Playing cards and billiards. (It's even better if you know any card tricks or how to do those cool trick shots we see on ESPN.)

- ❑ **g.** Bungee Jumping. (You can be called "The Comeback Kid.")
- ❑ **h.** All of the above.
- ❑ **i.** None of the above. If you've chosen none of the above, fill in the blank. I've got to be me, so I will ______________________.

NOTE

You won't be penalized if you make up your own answer. You may, however, be ridiculed by your family, staff, and friends if you choose a silly hobby. (Of course, they'll only do so behind your back. Once you are President, no one will ever tell you that you're doing something idiotic.)

CHECK YOUR WORK AND MAKE SURE YOU DIDN'T MAKE A FOOL OF YOURSELF.

TAKE A DEEP BREATH AND CONTINUE ON TO THE NEXT CHAPTER.

HEALTH:

Should I Cover My Mouth When I Cough Or Just Bury My Head in the Sand?

CHAPTER FIVE

BEFORE YOU DELVE into this chapter, it's important to know who the major players are in health administration.

POTUS Training Exercise #11

The government's answer to health issues and concerns is the Department of Health and Human Services (HHS), which is led by the Secretary. Yes, capital S. Don't be fooled by the humble title, the Secretary is the person responsible for leading all of HHS

and making critical decisions about health issues. (This Secretary does NOT get coffee and/or run errands for others.) The scope of the Secretary's responsibilities is breathtaking. (In fact, did you know that taking a breath falls under the responsibility of the Centers for Disease Control and Prevention (CDC)—and that its director gets paid $128,000 a year?) Many important health agencies fall under the HHS. Besides the CDC, the Food and Drug Administration (FDA), and the National Institutes of Health (NIH) all fall under the Secretary's aegis. But that's not all. This department is also responsible for policies on Medicare and Medicaid (M&M), counterterrorism, children, families, and tribal self-governance. That's why these people make top dollar. (Well . . . about $150,000.)

Are you beginning to understand how complicated a bureaucracy can be? If not, here's a little illustration.

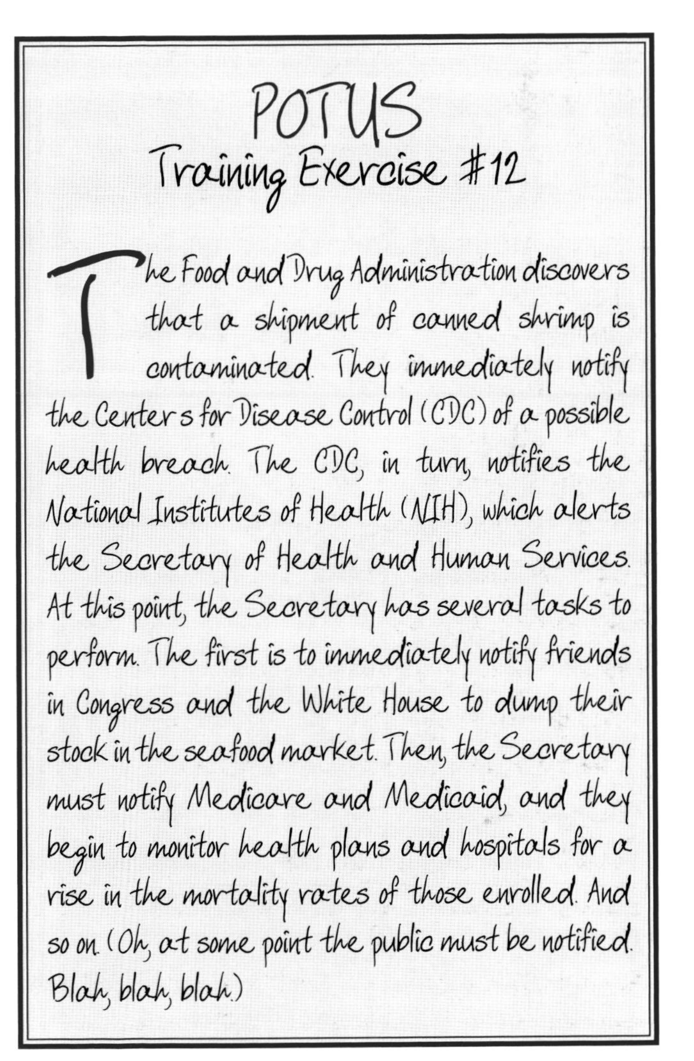

POTUS

Training Exercise #12

The Food and Drug Administration discovers that a shipment of canned shrimp is contaminated. They immediately notify the Centers for Disease Control (CDC) of a possible health breach. The CDC, in turn, notifies the National Institutes of Health (NIH), which alerts the Secretary of Health and Human Services. At this point, the Secretary has several tasks to perform. The first is to immediately notify friends in Congress and the White House to dump their stock in the seafood market. Then, the Secretary must notify Medicare and Medicaid, and they begin to monitor health plans and hospitals for a rise in the mortality rates of those enrolled. And so on. (Oh, at some point the public must be notified. Blah, blah, blah.)

GO ON TO THE NEXT PAGE

NOTE

Have you noticed how many acronyms we've used thus far in the chapter? Yes, the government is particularly fond of using acronyms. We realize that all these acronyms can be confusing for a government novice. In light of that, we decided to present you with a complete list/brief handbook of the most essential government acronyms. (We know this is the health chapter, but for informational purposes we also included acronyms that don't directly pertain to health.)

ACUITWH—Acronyms commonly used in the White House:

FYI—Follow your instincts. (Also known as "Oh, Jesus help me.")

POTUS—President of the United States. (You should know this by now.)

VPOTUS—Vice-President of the United States. (Makes sense, huh?)

FOPOTUS—Fraternal Order of Presidents of the United States.

HAFOPOTUS—Half-assed friends/relatives of the President.

COS—Chief of Staff. (Although COME—Chief of Manipulating Everything, is often used as well.)

ACIDD—Acronyms commonly invoked at the DOD—Department of Defense:

WMD—Welcome, my dear.

MIA—A mistake is an alternative.

IED—I'm extremely disappointed.

FEMA—Failure to evaluate much of anything.

DOHS—Department of Homeland Security and often used by the DOPES—Department of Preventing Evacuation and Services Personnel. (Yes there is a missing "P," but they didn't know where to find that either.)

TOP—Trailers on parade.

T&A—Trailers and accessories.

MRE—Millions of ridiculous experts.

TWO—Trailers without homes.

ITP—Isn't that pretentious?

MZ—Military zones.

LZ—Landing zones.

ZO—Zoned out.

ZIP—Zoning in Progress. (The context for this acronym is used with regard to Congressional redistricting or enabling real estate friends to make a killing in the market.)

AHHS—Acronyms pertaining to Health and Human Services:

HMO—While many people believe this has something to do with health care, that is only a consequence of its derivation. It originally meant, "**HEY MOE,**" referring to one of the Three Stooges. Moe understood that if you whacked someone over the head and tried to poke their eye out, they'd forget about any other ailment they might be suffering from.

ICU—Immediate Concern for Underwear. ICU now stands for a hospital's Intensive Care Unit, but for many, many years, it signified intensive concern for wearing clean underwear upon leaving your house. This has a direct connection with the old saying, "You never know

when you might get hit by a truck, so don't embarrass your mother by being caught dead in dirty underpants." The meaning changed when enough mortified mothers banded together and insisted on separate space for their rotten kids.

NIH—National Institute for the Helpless, not to be confused with **NIC**—the National Institute for the Capable.

ILB—Intolerable level of bullshit (used in every government agency to express frustration with political appointees).

STD—Some tedious dirt bags.

COD—Cures on demand.

DOC—Drugs of choice.

CLAP—Center for Losing All Patience. This is the place where civil servants are sent after having to deal with political appointees. The frustrated are referred here after serving in as few as one Democratic or Republican administration. Here, you might also find the **CLASH**—Center for Locating an Abundance of Stupid Humans.

ICE—While this acronym can mean In Case of Emergency, it is also used by the **DOHS**—To disguise an office so secret, they don't even know if they have a mission, what their mission is, and who is supposed to carry out this mission. It's so secret that it is almost impossible to find out where it is but

GO ON TO THE NEXT PAGE

what we have learned is that the office is disguised as Immigration, Customs, and Eliminations (or is it evaluations?), and it's conveniently located close enough to Cuba to avoid an invasion.

Now that we've totally cleared up the mystery of acronyms, let's get back to the questions.

Health History

110. Did you have sex before marriage? (Remember, this IS our business.) ____________________

111. Have you had sex since marriage? ____________

112. Is it likely that your sexual escapades will become fodder for a hungry media? ____________________

113. Is it likely that you will make your opponent's sex history fodder for a hungry media? (This is very important because we must know if the campaign will be interesting enough to watch on the nightly news.) ____________

114. Have you ever denied smoking marijuana, snorting cocaine, using barbiturates, or choking on an uncoated as-

pirin? You may think this is silly but the denial is always much more amusing than the admission. ____________

115. Body language and vocal responses play a large part in how the public will interpret your inner feelings. Facial movements, as you know, play an integral part in your body image. If your mother's warning to "take that stupid expression off your face or it will freeze that way," comes to fruition, and your face does freeze, it would certainly have an impact on your health. It is therefore imperative for you to decide which facial expressions are suitable for which situations. Which of the following choices are you most comfortable with?

- ❑**a.** Shedding no tears. You never want to be perceived as anything but restrained.
- ❑**b.** Shedding only one tear when being asked to comment about the loss of life due to a national tragedy. That single tear, along with a slight bowing of the head and uttering of a phrase like "my heart goes out to them" can project the image of a compassionate and caring President.
- ❑**c.** Shedding tears down both cheeks, while wringing your hands and moaning, "My God. Oh my God." People may perceive you as being hysterical, and possibly even out of control, but they will also empathize with your pain.

GO ON TO THE NEXT PAGE

116. In order to see if you can think on your feet (while facing the possibility of frozen-face syndrome), which of the following would best fit your press conference persona? Use as an example of a situation the unlikely case of being asked about rebuilding a city after a natural disaster of the hurricane variety.

❑**a.** Showing a grimace, which would indicate the enormity of the task, while avoiding putting your hands on your stomach. If you're seen rubbing your stomach and slightly moaning, the media might think you need to go to the bathroom.

❑**b.** Nodding your head in agreement as though you already have the solution. Then smiling, snapping your fingers, and saying while looking at the camera, "Life without jazz is no life at all."

❑**c.** Putting a little smirk on your face, moving your head from side to side (as though you're in tune with your favorite song, "Sitting on the Dock of the Bay") and responding with, "It's the Governor's problem. I refuse to violate any state's rights."

❑**d.** Showing a look of surprise, staring straight in the eyes of the reporter, and chuckling while saying, "Why rebuild anything? Let's just move everyone to states with few Congressional districts and a need for more—Republicans/Democrats."

(Select your party of choice. You should know by now which one since you already answered that question in Part One.)

117. The Secretary of Health and Human Services says that, "As a world we're not prepared for a pandemic." As the POTUS, you'll have to reevaluate your priorities. Which do you think is more important for the government to fund?

- ❑**a.** A vaccine for the chicken flu.
- ❑**b.** A self-tanning cream to avoid constant exposure to the sun's deadly rays.
- ❑**c.** A vaccine for the turkey flu. (That's right, several turkeys have died.)
- ❑**d.** A vaccine for the donut flu. (In the end, obesity is the country's biggest problem.)

As the POTUS, your job is not only to lead the free world, but to save it as well. (At least long enough for the next POTUS to be elected and deal with the long-term environmental issues.) With that in mind, please answer the next set of questions.

118. Do you think that certain species should be endangered?____

119. Do you think that certain types of people should be endangered? ___________________

120. Do you know how to endanger a species? ________

121. How do you warm a globe? ________________

122. Have you EVER considered buying an electronic globe that shows where every country is located (the Internet is flat and globes are round, so don't tell me you can access this online), what products they produce, how many people have lived through famine and plague, and how much money you need to allocate to them in order for them to call us their friend? ________________

123. Some people believe global warming is causing glaciers to melt at a rapid speed. What would you advise people to do about this?

- ❑ **a.** Buy a beachfront property in Ohio.
- ❑ **b.** Throw their mother's hairspray away.
- ❑ **c.** Read only information published by experts who say there is no global warming.
- ❑ **d.** Turn off your lights, the television, the computer, and everything else that uses electricity. Sit in the dark. Jewish mothers can tell you how to do this most effectively.

❑ **e.** Encourage people to either recycle cans, bottles, plastic bags, and newspapers, or stop reading, cooking, and drinking.

❑ **f.** Before cutting deals with foreign friends, insist they adhere to strict codes of improving the environment. Why should we have to suffer?—Let someone else do it.

124. Do you really believe that global warming is a problem? Or do you want to scream, "Give me a break!" ______

125. If global warming really is that bad, don't you think people wouldn't be rushing to live in the Southern states? ______

126. Do you believe that global warming is nothing more than a rumor started by politicians in blue states as an attempt to keep their constituents from moving to red states?

____

127. Do you think that toxic-waste dumps and dumping toxic waste are federal issues? ______________

128. Do you believe that waste dumps can be used by the Homeland Defense Department to test new biological weapons against terrorists? (This can actually be beneficial for the country. In case of a pandemic, these dumps could provide a ring of toxic waste around large cities, keeping

GO ON TO THE NEXT PAGE

high-tax-paying citizens in, while keeping out people who aren't immunized.) ______________________________

129. How would you respond to a media question about big corporations dumping toxic waste into clean water sources?

- ❑**a.** "Of course our hearts and prayers go out to all people who live in that area. But there's no need to make a federal case of it!"
- ❑**b.** "These people are my friends. They give to charity, pray to God, and most importantly, they have supported every campaign I've waged . . . I mean run in. They would never do anything that naughty. In fact, right now, I'm going to issue a mandate to all pharmaceutical companies to ensure we have the right stuff on hand to prevent any medical problems that may arise."
- ❑**c.** "We'll have the EPA keep a close eye on that water source to make sure no one drinks from it."
- ❑**d.** "Liar, liar, pants on fire."

130. We've decided to put the question about homeless people under the environment section of this test because, let's face it, they do clutter up the space outside of our homes. Homelessness is a serious issue. Which of the following statements would you use to call attention to the plight of the homeless in a real and meaningful way?

- ❑**a.** "We need to help the homeless people in Florida who are wandering around seriously confused because, while they're always ready for a hurricane, they don't expect it to be cold in January."
- ❑**b.** "If you want to help the homeless, you need to put your aluminum cans in a clearly marked container that says, 'Homeless help yourselves.' Remember to separate it from the rest of your recyclables."
- ❑**c.** "People must unite in their effort to find the homeless a home, whether it be on the range, in a city, or in a military desperate for more troops."

CHECK YOUR WORK AND MAKE SURE YOU DIDN'T MAKE A FOOL OF YOURSELF.

TAKE A DEEP BREATH AND CONTINUE ON TO THE NEXT CHAPTER.

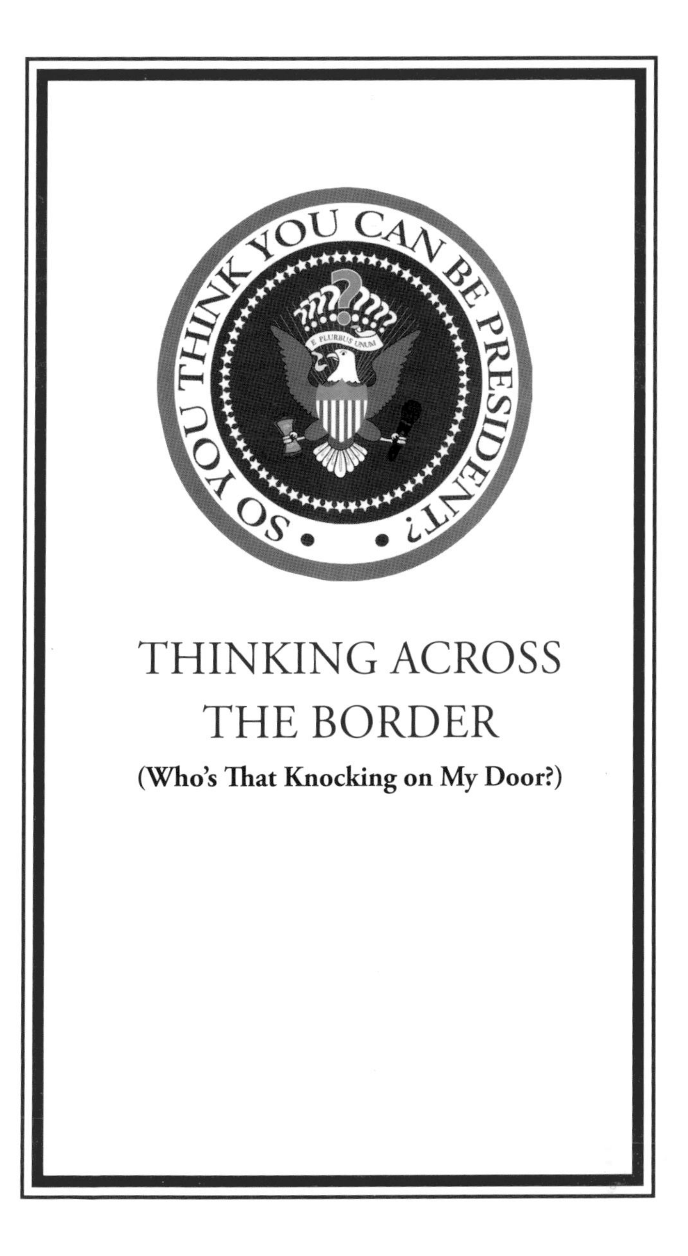

THINKING ACROSS THE BORDER

(Who's That Knocking on My Door?)

CHAPTER SIX

THE GROWING NUMBER of illegal immigrants is an important issue to Americans.

Some Americans may be all for letting any- and everyone onto our illustrious streets of gold, but many may feel that our streets are already too crowded with people who can't, or won't, speak English. (Although, if crowding is the problem here, why can't we just send immigrants to the Midwest? Don't they have miles and miles of uninhabited land?) It may seem strange that immigration is such an issue to Americans since our country began with a bunch of stuffy English immigrants, but times have changed and gone are the days when immigrants were welcomed at our ports with open arms. Now Americans remain wary of foreigners (legal or illegal) who could potentially steal their jobs by accepting a smaller salary.

In order to ease their concerns, you, as President, will meet with a number of ethnic organizations to discuss immigration. This is always a good idea because it demonstrates that you are not afraid of people who are different. (We mean "different" in the nicest possible way.) This could also be perceived as a bad idea because the public may feel that you are siding with the "other" folk. This next section will assess your ability to deal with the immigration issue in a diplomatic fashion.

✎ **131.** Are you related to someone who does not speak English? ______________________________

132. How many people work for US Customs and Borders Protection (CBP)? (Too hard? Okay, it's 42,000.) ________

133. If you took everyone who works for CBP out of their offices and put them on the borders, do you believe they would actually be doing our country a service?________

134. Have you ever met anyone who had a J visa or an F visa? If not, how will you decide who gets what visa and how long they will stay in this country? Okay, you got us, the POTUS doesn't have to decide. So, who should have that job in government?

- ❑ **a.** Someone who frequently eats in a Greek diner where the staff is entirely Hispanic.

❑b. Someone who eats at an Italian restaurant where the entire staff is from Pakistan.

❑c. Someone who has employed a multitude of au pairs from many different nations.

Answer the following questions "true" or "false":

135. Do the 42,000 people employed by US Customs and Border Protection work?____________________

136. How many of the 42,000 are fluent in a second language and what is the language? ____________________

NOTE

Too difficult again? All 42,000 people who work for CBP are fluent in a second language.

137. Is the language English? ____________________

138. The original settlers of the US did not intend to become a gated community (or maybe they did). All Americans are descendants of immigrants from another country, with the exception of Native American Indians. Which of

GO ON TO THE NEXT PAGE

the following programs would you consider as a solution for the lame, sick, and poor who demand entrance?

❑**a.** Remove all border personnel and restrictions. Instead, place a large sign on each entrance with a list of do's and don'ts. (Remember to have those signs printed in several languages.)

❑**b.** Give all immigrants full status, including education and medical benefits. Diluting the border patrol and making them language teachers can offset the costs of doing this. The INS courts and judges can also be liquidated, since eliminating the people will eliminate the cost of that paper work as well. (If you remove the volatile topic of immigration, you'll also be removing ammunition that your opponents can use in the next election.)

❑**c.** Devise a plan where immigrants are moved into "developed" areas where no citizen wants to live. The policy worked for Native Americans, and now they have gambling casinos. (As we said earlier, you should really consider the Midwest thing.)

139. One of the biggest costs of controlling and guiding a multilingual country comes from the need to have all information, rules, and regulations printed, posted, and spoken in a large number of different languages. Which of

the following options do you think can feasibly solve this problem once and for all?

- ❑**a.** Create a new common language and make classes mandatory for all immigrants. This will not eliminate the language problem, but it'll make it easier to identify the people who want to take over American jobs.
- ❑**b.** Transform the written word into pictures. European countries have done this for many years. They simply use a combination of circles, squares, and images to depict the meanings of words. For example, a picture of a toilet and an arrow indicates a "tinkle stop."
- ❑**c.** Create a national language translating service on the Internet. For a small fee, all one has to do is log in and have their communications translated into the required language. As a side benefit, the National Security Agency will have full access to all communications. This way, they won't have to get legal permission to spy.

140. What is the "wet foot, dry foot" policy?

- ❑**a.** It's a policy that applies to Cuban immigrants who forget their flippers when they leave home.

GO ON TO THE NEXT PAGE

❑**b.** It is a national secret. (You'll never know without top secret clearance . . . unless you are a member of the Cuban National Foundation.)

❑**c.** It's a dance step used by choreographers south of Georgia and west of NYC.

❑**d.** It's an annual marathon sponsored by the fabulous Florida Keys.

141. How many different immigration card colors are there? Please circle all the immigration card colors you think exist.

❑**a.** Green—for immigrants who need working visas.

❑**b.** Periwinkle—for immigrants who are potential threats to heterosexuals.

❑**c.** Teal—for immigrants who are mentally challenged but are able to work in a port city.

❑**d.** Yellow—for immigrants who may be diseased by a chicken or a turkey.

❑**e.** Rose—for immigrants who are complete morons but will dress nicely for work.

❑**f.** Black—for immigrants who are probably suicide bombers.

❑**g.** Brown—for the White House domestic help.

Making Decisions About Homeland Security

Everyone agrees that patriotism is good. From its name alone, it seems reasonable to assume that everyone agrees that the Patriot Act is good. Wrong. The country may love feeling all warm, safe, and protected in their homes, but they definitely don't love the Patriot Act. Forget the security of the country, let's hear it for protecting our civil liberties!

POTUS
Training Exercise #13

Being the sharp POTUS that you are, you know that the public will never understand that you know the best way to protect them and all their friends from terrorists, pornographic e-mails, and phony phone calls. But as a President who knows how important ratings are, you must somehow reconcile the need to protect the country with the public's need to protect their freedoms. (What's wrong with these people? Everyone knows freedom isn't "free.")

This next section will discuss all the security issues that you face as the President. The questions will determine how you will deal with probing questions about security without letting on that:

1. You don't know the answer.
2. You aren't sure how to answer, since your own

administration has been breaking those annoying Constitutional rights.

3. You know the answer, but will lie to protect the country (as well as your administration).

If you can handle these questions with aplomb, then you'll surely be able to handle America's demanding questions, while saving your own behind.

142. Can you define "homeland"?__________________

143. Have you ever been to an airport in your homeland? __________________________________

144. Have you ever had to take your computer out of the case, your shoes off your feet, your change out of your pockets, and admit to wearing an underwire bra in order to allow someone to feel you up?____________________

145. Do you have a personal crisis plan? ______________

146. Would you share your plan with the American people? ____________________________________

147. Did you write it yourself or did your mom do it because she was concerned about what would happen if they rushed you out of the White House?__________________

148. Would you share your mother with the American people? ________________________________

149. What can you do when the actions of a few impact the welfare of the many? Below you'll find a dialogue involving things that may be considered questionable and illegal. (Remember, as President, you must protect the nation from itself—you know what's right and good.) Look carefully at the following Q&A discourse. Do you find it to be:

- ❑**a.** Plausible.
- ❑**b.** Acceptable.
- ❑**c.** Immoral, unethical, backwards, and naïve.
- ❑**d.** A guide for how you will answer all controversial questions in the future.

Q: Mr./Ms. President, will you continue to secretly tap telephones even though it's illegal?
A: Certainly not. Everyone whose phone calls are to be recorded will receive a registered letter indicating that we will be tapping into their phone and telling them when.
Q: Although wiretapping is illegal and pretty much useless, what if it's determined that there's an ongoing foreign conspiracy underfoot and a national terrorist strike similar to 9/11 is expected?
A: Well, we'll need to tap the phones of everyone who doesn't live in the United States. However, since a President's

GO ON TO THE NEXT PAGE

most positive poll numbers are usually after a national crisis, we should also consider allowing an attack as a way to unite the country. And, of course, to boost my ratings.

150. There have been oh-so-many suggestions about how to keep people safe. We have security on airplanes, at shopping malls, in apartment buildings, and at places of business. How will you make sure people are safe at home, at work, or at play?

- ❑ **a.** Require people to present identification before entering someone's home or office. Everyone knows that terrorists never carry identification, and even if they do, they will make a big fuss about not showing it.
- ❑ **b.** Make sure no one is allowed to take pictures of bridges or tunnels. Everyone has seen a bridge before, so why take pictures?
- ❑ **c.** Ban bringing backpacks into sports stadiums or knives onto planes. Of course, people can carry all kinds of firearms, but that is neither here nor there (nor a part of this question).
- ❑ **d.** Get rid of all civil liberties. Security can't be compromised just because people think the Constitution is important.
- ❑ **e.** Implement a national curfew, such as a lockdown at sunset. Only terrorists will violate the curfew and law-enforcement personnel who have

nothing else to do will surely be able to identify them.

❑f. Stagger days for when ethnic groups are allowed to shop.

❑g. Capture potential terrorists by offering discounts on products they are likely to buy, like diesel fuel, black powder, disposable cell phones, grenade launchers, assault weapons, a how-to-make-a-thirty-minute-bomb kit, kabobs, tahini, and pita sandwiches.

❑h. Close down libraries or bookstores that carry books about making incendiary devices or building a doll house.

151. Without infringing on their civil liberties, what will you do to protect the people of this great nation?

❑a. Place telephone booths all around the country with signs that say: CONFIDENTIAL CALLING ONLY, with additional signs assuring people that these phones will not be bugged or recorded. If there is a question as to why someone would want to use these phones, you can take their picture and follow them home.

❑b. Advertise a new cell phone on television that has a built-in spy-zapper that prohibits anyone from listening in. Of course, since you'll already have their credit card info and home address, it

should be easy enough to have a law officer move in next door and put an ear to their window.

❑c. Stand under the eaves of a potential terrorist's house and hope that the only thing that drops from above is some information.

152. It's extremely important for security designations to be clear, consistent, and always implemented. The following are security classifications. Please list them in order of importance, with one being the most important.

❑a. Official Use Only: The classification for parking lot attendants who protect the anonymity of cars reserved for VIP spaces while visiting the Pentagon.

❑b. Confidential: The classification for the hundreds of employees who typed up the parking lot reservations by name.

❑c. Secret: The classification for gossipy information about the employees who typed up those lists.

❑d. Top Secret: The classification for any visiting VIPs and the exact purpose of any meeting. For example, was it for a social visit, illegal lobbying, or to write government legislation?

Let's tackle another "hypothetical" scenario.

POTUS

Training Exercise #14

Imagine that a national disaster has occurred. It doesn't matter if the disaster is a flood, famine, or red death—it's your choice. Thousands of people have been forced to leave their homes, businesses, families, pets, and friends. Not to worry, the Department of Homeland Security/FEMA acts immediately and spends billions of dollars to house all the displaced people. They purchase RVs and find temporary hotel accommodations in non-disaster areas. Then you find out that, for whatever reason, the vehicle and hotel accommodations will not be able to accommodate folks up until they can find other homes or have their homes repaired or get a check from FEMA. ("Why?" is always a bureaucratic question that will never be answered, so don't waste your time on things that are only in your imagination.) If this wasn't bad enough, another

GO ON TO THE NEXT PAGE

disaster is about to befall the area and everyone must move on before it hits. Then you discover that about 11,000 trailers stand empty in some obscure Arkansas town ironically called Hope.

153. What would you instruct the Director of FEMA to do to facilitate finding places for people to live and start new lives? Put the following list of alternatives in order of priority:

- ❑**a.** Plant trees and bushes near the unoccupied trailers.
- ❑**b.** Buy thousands of bus tickets to Hope.
- ❑**c.** Register all the displaced people as Democrats and then give them free tickets to the Clinton Library. A refugee who receives a free gift is a happier refugee.
- ❑**d.** Buy thousands of sleep sofas.
- ❑**e.** Buy thousands of chocolate bars.
- ❑**f.** Develop a friendship with any big timeshare company.
- ❑**g.** Turn the trailers into green houses where you can grow hallucinogenic substances. People may not even notice the disaster, or at least it won't be as unpleasant.
- ❑**h.** Provide free galoshes, penicillin, rafts, cans of foam, and anti-pestilence cream.

- ❑ **i.** Provide inflatable houseboats for a flood emergency.
- ❑ **j.** Make sure each house trailer comes with a moving truck.
- ❑ **k.** Assign a 5,000-gallon tanker truck to be available for every hundred trailer trucks. You don't want anyone running out of gas as they flee from a second impending disaster.
- ❑ **l.** Ensure that each trailer comes with a Coast Guard-approved survival gearbox, including a raft and a GPS location device. (Maybe you might want to remove those survival knives from the kits.)
- ❑ **m.** Send in the BSA—Boy Scouts of America—to set up tents and barbeque pits. (Don't make the mistake of sending the Girl Scouts of America. They'll only tidy up the tents and try to sell cookies.)

CHECK YOUR WORK AND MAKE SURE YOU DIDN'T MAKE A FOOL OF YOURSELF.

TAKE A DEEP BREATH AND CONTINUE ON TO THE NEXT CHAPTER.

DEFENSE AND VETERANS

(Or, Why Do You Need Two Buildings to Deal with the Same People? Or, How Can a Person Be 100% Disabled and Still Be Alive? Or, How Come the Administrator Wears Suits but the Surgeon General Has a Uniform?)

CHAPTER SEVEN

THE ISSUE OF defense is always a touchy subject for the President, primarily because the Department of Defense budget is always controversial. People just don't realize how much money it takes to defend this country, even if no one is invading us . . . yet. As the leader of our illustrious Department of Defense, you'll have to find creative ways to explain not only your immense budget for stuff like guns and flip-flops (soldiers need their feet to breathe in those hot countries, you know), but you'll also need to defend your actions. (We're sure that if you give an order to shoot everyone, you have a good reason.)

This is also why it's imperative for military secrets to stay secrets. Not only is it important not to alert enemy countries to our defense strategies, it's also important to hide your mess-ups and bad decisions from the public. But, as we all know, most secrets have a way of coming out. As President, it's also your job to ensure that only inconsequential secrets are leaked out. This way the public will be too involved in being up in arms about those trivial secrets while your most covert secrets remain safe from prying eyes.

It is imperative to make sure military secrets stay secrets. Which of the answers to the following questions would you make sure remain classified?

154. Who is the Secretary of Defense? ______________

155. Who is the Secretary of Offense? ______________

156. How many people work for the Department of Defense (DOD)? ______________

157. How many are political appointees? ______________

158. How many are civilians? ______________

159. How many are military? ______________

160. How many of the people who fill military positions want to kill the civilians?______________

161. How many have good cause and will not be prosecuted to the full extent of the law in either a military court or by kangaroos?______________

162. What are the things you need to know before hiring a Secretary of Defense? Please decide if the following statements are important in your selection. A simple "yes" or "no" will suffice.

❑**a.** Someone being hired for that position should be an expert in defense, not offense. Offense falls to the Vice-President.

❑**b.** Potential applicants should be stripped to see if they have any jailhouse tattoos, which would indicate that they are familiar with defending themselves (which can mean that they will be able to defend themselves against the media or against an enemy country). In addition, they are accustomed to standing for long periods.

❑**c.** Individuals who have felony criminal records should not be eliminated just because they're naughty. The power of your office allows you to issue pardons; this may be the time to use it.

❑**d.** Individuals whom you are considering must be forbidden to work long hours in order to prevent planning a coup. (You can head this off by always making sure you give them a little something extra in their budget.)

GO ON TO THE NEXT PAGE

163. It is essential that the Commander-in-Chief understand how DOD money is spent. Which of the following statements is true?

- ❑**a.** In fiscal year 2006, the House passed a $700 billion appropriations bill for the Defense Department.
- ❑**b.** Sumo wrestler suits are important elements in developing international understanding, so it's imperative for the army to keep them on hand.
- ❑**c.** Along with purchasing sumo wrestler suits, the Air Force maintains a supply of white china plates. (You never know when an emergency dinner for 8,000 people will pop up.)
- ❑**d.** A legitimate military expenditure is importing sand to Saudi Arabia.
- ❑**e.** The Pentagon recently disposed of $33 billion worth of excess equipment, all of which was unused or in excellent condition.
- ❑**f.** Important wartime expenditures include bingo consoles, espresso machines, and golf memberships.

164. The White House is always called upon to defend military expenditures. As Commander-in-Chief, how can you continue to spend and waste while satisfying public outcry for savings? Choose from the following options.

❑**a.** Create a "Department of Waste" which protects and defends the government's imprudent and wasteful spending. (It would be easy to bury the Defense spending here.)

❑**b.** Challenge the public to find better uses for the money within the DOD bureaucracy, and then make sure all the information they need to meet the challenge is classified or unavailable.

❑**c.** Produce a TV program called *The Terrorist or You*, where a team of civilian contestants battles military contestants over the DOD budget. While it would appear that the civilian team has equal opportunity for victory, the consequences of any answer they give results in a terrorist take-over in their neighborhood.

165. The Secretary of Defense is solely responsible for developing and submitting a budget to Congress. What advice would you give to your Secretary in order to make some "out of the box" budget cuts?

❑**a.** Eliminate the title Secretary—that phrase still makes most men wince anyway—as well as any variations of it such as Under-, Deputy-, or If Everyone Else Dies Secretary from the US Army, Air Force, and Navy. (And if you wonder why we didn't mention the US Marine Corps, you better hit the books. They are part of the US

GO ON TO THE NEXT PAGE

Navy.) These positions are useless and, at times, vacant for a long period. Aside from the Plum Book and the Congress, no one knows these jobs even exist.

❑ **b.** Eliminate the entire US Air Force. Their primary role is transporting troops and cargo. Wouldn't it be more beneficial to lease bankrupt commercial airlines? You would eliminate the need for medical benefits and cute uniforms.

❑ **c.** Convince the Salvation Army to join forces with the DOD, which will certainly cut costs. Its portable soup kitchens and abundance of donated clothing would be perfect assets for Special Operations personnel. Besides, the Salvation Army lacks a real General and this would be the perfect way to entice them into agreeing to a joint venture.

❑ **d.** Ask the INS to turn all captured illegal immigrants over to the DOD, and then use them in the Armed Forces (except direct combat support). Putting them on the Defense payroll and adding an additional surcharge to their wages would reduce the national debt.

166. The Secretary of Defense also has the responsibility of keeping our nation in a Patriotic mood. Old slogans used during the Vietnam War, like, "It's not much of a war

but it's all we got," didn't set the right tone, so extreme care has to be taken when trying to create a warlike attitude. To keep with the concept that "the President is always right," the use of television, movies, books, slogans, endorsements by well-known movie stars (like John Wayne, whom we recently discovered is still making movies disguised as George Clooney), and other mind-altering literature is necessary. With all that in mind, which of the following choices should the Secretary adopt to project a Patriotic image to the American people?

- ❑**a.** Wearing a steel helmet, body armor, and sporting a pair of ivory-handled Colt .45s.
- ❑**b.** Riding in a Bradley Fighting Tank rather than a stretch limousine. Your security detachment would travel in either Humvees or assault helicopters. Equipping choppers with loud speakers that play patriotic music, like "Don't Step on My Blue Suede Boots," "Forever in Fatigues," and "Born in the USA."
- ❑**c.** Endorsing some of the top riders in the PBR (Professional Bull Riders) circuit. That kind of exposure will convey the message that any bull can be controlled and handled.
- ❑**d.** Change the All-Volunteer Force into a true all-volunteer force. If they love America so much, they should be able to serve without pay or benefits. (Then we'll know who the true patriots are.)

GO ON TO THE NEXT PAGE

This section will test how you'll react to international emergencies. Be advised that this part of the examination is designated as confidential. (Remember the "eyes only" classification?) We promise that your answers will not be released to the public, so don't try to give the answers you think you should give. We have ways of knowing if your selection doesn't match your personality and character. Reply based on your instincts.

167. You are snatched out of your bed by Secret Service agents and told that our country has been invaded from the South. What's the first thing you'd do?

- ❑**a.** Call your Secretary of Defense and order him to start shooting anyone who looks Hispanic.
- ❑**b.** Grab your most prized possessions, run out to your awaiting helicopter on the South Lawn, and fly to Canada.
- ❑**c.** Using your "hands-only" red cell, contact your mother, give her your 7-8 (that's secret talk for location), and make sure she calls your spouse to apologize for your leaving her/him behind.
- ❑**d.** You put your clothes on. No one can take any decision a naked President makes seriously.

168. After fleeing to your secret command post outside of Ontario, you're told that there was a mistake in the communiqué about the invasion. The only thing invading the South was the "Citrus Canker," which was destroying the key-lime trees in South Florida. (Damn the Department of Agriculture and their ominous emails!) What can you do to rectify your horrible mistake?

- ❑**a.** Return to the White House, apologize on national television, and tell everyone that you made an honest mistake and that your prayers are with all those brave Hispanics who have lost their lives. (Have Trini Lopez singing "If I Had a Hammer" in the background.)
- ❑**b.** Announce a budget package that will reimburse funeral expenses and give compensatory damages to the victim's families. (Not to exceed $100 per family.)
- ❑**c.** Have FEMA immediately place trailers and RVs into those areas where houses were burnt or where farms were destroyed. (Yes, the Secretary was certainly thorough.) If trailers aren't available, relocate people to hotels, but only for a limited amount of time.
- ❑**d.** Announce a national prayer day and declare a national holiday to celebrate the tragedy. It could be called "La Vida Loca." Translation: "The Crazy Life."

GO ON TO THE NEXT PAGE

169. You get an urgent message from your Secretary of Defense relaying that a Middle Eastern nation has declared a civil war. What course of action would you use to demonstrate understanding, care, and concern?

- ❑**a.** Order US troops throughout the world to lay down their weapons and light candles of hope. Explain that bringing "civility" to war is a lot better than shooting and bombing each other.
- ❑**b.** Do a quick poll to find out which side has the most voting constituents in this country and have US troops start wearing that flag on their uniforms.
- ❑**c.** Offer those loyal to America an "associate-member status" with the United States, which would guarantee free medical care for their parents.

170. The Department of Defense has always strived to keep the safety and comfort of the troops as its number one priority. This is why troops deployed around the world are supplied with equipment and uniforms that accommodate the geographical peculiarities of whichever terrain they are in. For example, soldiers in Vietnam found that their leather boots rotted, so the military replaced them with "jungle" boots. Following that example, which of the following choices should the military institute?

- ❑**a.** All troops fighting in the desert should wear sandals.

- ❑ **b.** All sailors should wear flippers.
- ❑ **c.** All troops stationed in New York should wear tap shoes.
- ❑ **d.** All troops in Holland must have wooden shoes.
- ❑ **e.** Anyone serving at an embassy should have black patent-leather pumps.
- ❑ **f.** If posted in France, ballet shoes must be requisitioned.
- ❑ **g.** In tropical areas, a nice pair of flip-flops should be supplied.

FACTOID: It was discovered that troops fighting in urban areas suffered a high casualty rate. The DOD determined that there was a need for a more complete and state of the art body protection. Military research and development issued new protective equipment but still the casualty rate steadily increased. Turns out that troops were dying not from enemy fire, but from heat strokes caused by their body armor.

GO ON TO THE NEXT PAGE

171. The Senate Committee on Veterans Affairs at Capitol Hill recently approved S. 1182, which allows using money from the VA's healthcare budget to study outsourcing VA healthcare jobs. The study, with VA healthcare funds going to private consultants, could cost over $140 million and lead to the loss of up to 36,000 VA jobs. How would you insist the Veterans Affairs leader handle this situation?

- ❑**a.** Create an online, self-help, chat room where initial claims for disability can be diagnosed, thereby reducing the number of doctors required.
- ❑**b.** Create regional temporary medical housing using unused FEMA mobile homes.
- ❑**c.** Convert existing VA hospitals into recreational timeshares for the general public and staff them with disqualified applicants. At least they'll get free room and board.
- ❑**d.** Establish a timetable for reducing VA disability benefits. For example, how can a person receive a 100% disability if they can submit an application? Something's fishy about that.
- ❑**e.** Install a virus into any application that is being submitted to really see how bad people want disability.

172. In the history of senior officials at the Veterans Administration, there have been some real warriors, while some have had ongoing political appointments. If asked to appoint someone for that important Cabinet position, what kind of person would you consider?

- ❑a. Someone who has all of their marbles, but only some of their body parts.
- ❑b. A former ambassador to a religious area like Jerusalem or the Holy See. (No, it's not an ocean.)
- ❑c. Someone with no military experience but who is well connected with Beltway lobbyists, who will whine (the spelling is intentional), dine, and lobby to never cut the Secretary's entertainment budget.

173. Which of the following labor-resolving solutions would you implement in the best interest of the American people?

- ❑a. Institute covert wiretapping on both the worker and management leaders to find out who really is the bad guy. Then target them as al-Qaeda affiliated and send them to Cuba.
- ❑b. Make it mandatory to have tip jars placed in every location where a worker comes into contact with the public they serve. Declare it as nontaxable money, to be used for future secret surveillance projects.
- ❑c. Have all striking employees dip their fingers (all four plus thumb) into a bright orange ink

that never washes off. They'll always be easy to identity, especially to those whom they've caused incredible difficulties for.

❑**d.** Go on national TV and announce that it's time for both sides to show some leadership and get 'er done. To show your trust in them, you're going elk hunting in Yellowstone National Park before all the grizzlies eat all the elk up.

174. How many people does it take to change a light bulb?

____

175. Have you ever changed a light bulb? __________

176. Do you have at least ten friends in the energy supply business who will make considerable profits from any decisions you make? ______________________________

177. Are you concerned with how much gas the Presidential limo (as well as other Presidential vehicles) uses when the President goes anywhere? _____________________

178. If elected, would you consider giving up your gas-guzzling Presidential limo in favor of a hybrid? (Don't use the excuse that a hybrid isn't secure. You're the President, the automobile industry will do what ever you want. That's

why it's nice to be President. But you knew that, which is why you're taking this test.) ____________________

179. Do you think that sports activities like NASCAR (that's where fancy fast cars keep going around in circles until one of them finally crashes or crosses the finish line) should be outlawed because they waste fuel? If no, why not?

- ❑**a.** It's a beloved American pastime.
- ❑**b.** The participants are big political contributors.
- ❑**c.** It sends a message to the rest of the world that everything is just fine and dandy in the USA.

180. As President, you'll probably always travel in a limo. But what if you owned a bus? (Imagine Air Force One, but on the road; like something Kelly Clarkson travels in.) What measures—on or off the bus—would you take to ensure that it's compatible with the environment? Which of the following choices makes the most sense to you?

- ❑**a.** Insist that only Willie Nelson's biodiesel fuel be used. Of course, you'll also need a tow truck that runs on regular fuel to follow you when you venture north of Georgia and the fuel in your bus turns to Jell-O. Realistically, this may limit your outreach to only citizens in the

GO ON TO THE NEXT PAGE

South and your listening to only cow-poking music. But isn't that why God invented satellite communication?

❑b. Eliminate any possibility of putrid, green, smelly cleanser escaping into a forest or a lake by never flushing the toilet on board. When you're in or near a major American city, you can flush away.

❑c. Find an Amish chap who can convert and modify your bus so it can be pulled by a team of sixteen mules. It would ultimately be a perpetual-motion wagon train, a sensible approach to energy conservation and saving the environment. Then have another bus follow behind to scrape up all the droppings. (If this doesn't work, run him over. You don't want him to start a movement. The Amish have no telephones and no fast vehicles. You, on the other hand, have unimaginable resources—they'll never catch you.)

FACTOID: There is no gold in Fort Knox. All that remains in those vaults are old promissory notes from foreign countries, Amtrak, and two past Presidents.

181. If an unusual natural disaster were to occur, what would your first thoughts be?

❏a. What actions do I need to take to protect my approval rating?

❏b. Should I look into the possibility of forming a subdivision that focuses only on catastrophes we haven't dealt with in the past? Like flocks of wild chickens running around helter-skelter and infecting upon everyone they come into contact with a deadly virus. Maybe I should appoint someone to be the Official Chicken Catcher.

❏c. If there is the possibility of massive injuries and death due to illegally imported snakefish and killer bees, should I suggest that citizens stock their homes with duct tape because it could be converted into bee paper, just like in the days of old? Or should I suggest the use of killer bees as bait for the snakefish? (Using them will greatly increase the cost effectiveness in eradicating both threats.)

182. If there's a normal natural disaster such as an earthquake, flood, hurricane, or tornado, what would you tell the public?

❏a. It's just Mother Nature's way of expressing herself.

❏b. There, but for the Grace of God, go I! Let it work itself out.

GO ON TO THE NEXT PAGE

- ❑ **c.** The only response from the federal government will be a National Day of Prayer.

183. What would you, as the newly elected President, do to correct what appear to be somewhat shortsighted, malfunctioning, shameful feats of engineering in possible disaster areas?

- ❑ **a.** Hire someone who has spent a lifetime studying the beaver and has at least a fundamental knowledge about why beaver dams outlast anything man-made.
- ❑ **b.** Establish new building codes, which require building swimming holes instead of cities in places that will be decimated by a Category Three hurricane.
- ❑ **c.** Hire one of Johnny Cash's siblings before building cities at sea level or below. "How high's the water, Mama?" should be the first question asked.
- ❑ **d.** Either remove the title Army from the Corps of Engineers or, even better, make everyone in the department take basic training. That way if they screw up you can call it treason and shoot them on the levee of their choice.

184. Once the hundreds of thousands of families who have been evacuated, separated, and lost in cyberspace are found, will you consider:

❑**a.** Using the same program that the Friends of Animals initiated years ago and begin inserting microchips in everyone when they are born.

❑**b.** Suggest to employers they do the same, beginning with the most important people and working their way down to the laborers.

NOTE

Laborers are easily replaced by illegal aliens.

❑**c.** Putting information on these chips, such as being an organ donor, having second language talents, and porn sites visited in the last year.

❑**d.** Think about selling all this information to those porn sites, credit card companies, the INS, the AARP, NRA, Homeland Security, and the Defense Department to help defray the costs of this program.

185. This next question is a little more complicated and has more options than previous disasters, or questions. If it's too much for you to comprehend, take a few days and come

back to it when you feel up to it. (Actually, we take that back. If this were real, and not just a test, any delays in response would result in you being in deep doo-doo.) That being made clear, what would you do if a disaster were starting to make the United States look like a third world nation?

- ❑ **a.** Declare the affected area(s) as top secret and confiscate any media videos.
- ❑ **b.** Try to tidy up all the places where you know there is going to be news coverage.
- ❑ **c.** Call the Prime Minister of India and ask how that country deals with disaster.
- ❑ **d.** Fantasize about the way you think things should look and have a press conference where you insist that your fantasy is the truth.
- ❑ **e.** Show a video of our National Guard making High Altitude Low Opening precision drops of self-contained and easily assembled kitchens.
- ❑ **f.** Order thousands of square feet of artificial turf to cover areas that will be shown on the news. You might also want to use inflatable housing and trees to try to polish the area a bit more.
- ❑ **g.** Ignore any controversy and seek assistance from the Boy Scouts of America. They could impart a more civilized and enjoyable way of living outdoors with their campfire and single-gender singalong activities.

❑**h.** Hold a press conference praising the American way of life, showing the completely devastated area being cleaned up by a large group of smiling people, who are whistling while they work, with a background of several American flags and crosses (in appropriate areas) being scattered in the debris.

NOTE Consider hiring part-time actors to play the workers. Convince them to work free by telling them they can use the video credit on their resumes.

CHECK YOUR WORK AND MAKE SURE YOU DIDN'T MAKE A FOOL OF YOURSELF.

TAKE A DEEP BREATH AND CONTINUE ON TO THE NEXT CHAPTER.

DON'T KNOW MUCH ABOUT HISTORY OR TRIGONOMETRY

(Or, Running for a Second Term)

CHAPTER EIGHT

OVER THE YEARS, there have been many political discussions about education. Some people believe that the public school system sucks and opt to send their children to private schools and charter schools. Some people believe that the school system is immoral, illicit, depraved, corrupt, full of bad ideas, and not a nice place for their children. Some people would rather isolate their children and educate them in their own living rooms. (Hey, if it works for celebrities . . .) As the POTUS, it will be your job to lead people out of the darkness of the dumb and into the light of the learned.

186. Choose from the following first steps you will take to make sure no child is left behind . . . to get run over by the school bus or an oncoming truck.

- ❑ **a.** Give every child a computer where they can access the Internet and start some kind of lucrative porn site.

❑ **b.** Make truancy a treasonous act and lock up all the parents who don't know where their children are after 5:00 PM.

❑ **c.** Give teaching positions to people who have had real life experiences and can enrich a student's ability to discover the realities of the world. We should employ white-collar criminals who were extraordinarily successful, but had the misfortune to get caught throwing excessively extravagant parties with money that wasn't theirs.

POTUS
Training Exercise #15

School boards are often responsible for developing policy for the local school system, which is part of that silly states' rights thing. Just FYI, states' rights are situations where the federal government can only stand with its nose pressed up against the window because some Governor or local elected official thinks they know more than a Washington bureaucrat about what's best for their state. Get it? The states have rights that outweigh decisions the federal government makes.

This isn't exactly an education issue, but it's still an important one. Besides, didn't we cleverly segue into this topic with the whole school-board thing?

187. As President, there are numerous ways to get back at those silly states. But only if you want to teach them a lesson or you feel the need for entertainment beyond causing giant traffic jams. Which of the following options would you chose?

- ❑ **a.** Unfunded federal mandates. This is where the federal government requires the states to do something, but then screws them when it comes to funding. And when the states don't comply, they won't get money for roads or homeland security agents.
- ❑ **b.** Passing laws that impact the economy of specific states. For example, you could pass a law that forbids a man to have more than one wife unless the one wife has no sense of humor and weighs over 300 pounds. This might have consequences in Utah, but not until the wife has reached puberty. (Have you ever noticed that young female Utahans are very thin, but as they get older they gain enormous amounts of weight? Do you think the older females eat the younger ones? Or does that happen only if they come from Tonga?)

GO ON TO THE NEXT PAGE

❑**c.** Copy the Favored Nations Act with a Favored States Act. If a state does not support you, they don't get Federal Funding for anything. You'll repeal the Interstate Transportation Act and charge tolls from those states when crossing through your declared Favorite States. (Of course, that revenue is given to your favored state.) When they are forced into bankruptcy, they'll open their arms to any suggestions you have.

❑**d.** Have the Homeland Security Secretary leak unfounded yet plausible terrorist threats for large cities in the states that do not belong to the Favored States Alumni. Every time a story is leaked, the city will have to respond with increased security. Sooner or later it will cause them to spend so much money they'll have to come begging for funds to stay solvent.

❑**e.** Have two applications printed up. A one-page form for Favored Nations with a single sentence, "Please indicate how much money you need and where you want the funds transferred." The other form will be for Disfavored Nations and be completely blank—because that's all they're going to get.

POTUS
Training Exercise #16

Over the years, the holiday season (not just religious holidays) has become complicated by the number of holidays that require celebration. In addition, some people feel their holidays have been either marginalized or ignored by the federal government. (You see why we skirted the religious thing? If you don't get it, you need to study the Constitution. We can't do everything.) It has been suggested that we should table federal holidays and let each secular entity declare what celebrations they want.

Can you imagine what an opportunity this would be for the Deputy of Research for Useless Information? Each entity would need its own calendar and own discounted shopping days, which would be great for the printing business and the economy. But what if a student celebrated someone else's holiday by skipping school? This brings us to corporal punishment.

GO ON TO THE NEXT PAGE

188. As President of the United States (I guess by now you've become an expert in "let's pretend"), which of the following issues have you been most curious about?

- ❑**a.** The movement that abolished corporal punishment in public schools, but not in private schools.
- ❑**b.** Who actually began to change the way teachers are allowed to discipline? That old adage "spare the rod, spoil the child" was probably one of the most valuable tools to insure our children paid attention in school. Just FYI, did you ever consider why all our Presidents went to private schools?
- ❑**c.** What made parents begin to think, "How can my child learn if they are embarrassed in front of their peers? We need to eliminate punishment in the classroom. We need to do away with the dunce hat." I'm sure you agree that everyone loved the dunce hat. It was one of the gentler and yet more successful punishments. It was certainly better then getting hung on a nail in the front of the room. Which, by the way, provided hours of classroom entertainment. Much better than TV.
- ❑**d.** Who were the framers of the "ban corporal punishment" movement and were they in any way related to the person who had one of the country's greatest marketing successes? What was that success you ask? A group of inventors were

floundering with an unknown device called a metal detector until someone suggested that perhaps their device could be placed in the biggest market of all, the public-school system. But to make it work students needed to start rebelling and forming their own gang systems. In order to trigger this revolution, rap music was created and became the mantra for all disenchanted young people. This can't be just a coincidence, can it?

189. It is commonly agreed that "the youth of today will become our future leaders." But do you think they are being properly prepared to assume leadership roles? Based on the information you have about education in this country, which of the following questions do you think they would not be able to answer?

❑**a.** Why does two plus two equal four?
❑**b.** Why are there only twenty-eight letters in the alphabet?
❑**c.** How many metal detectors does it take to change a light bulb?

FACTOID: Since the inception of "No Child Left Behind," a recent survey shows that five out of every three children has shown little improvement.

It's common knowledge that the first four years of a new Presidential administration are spent campaigning to get elected for a second term. Although seldom thought of as a powerful entity, the person you pick to be the Secretary of the Department of Agriculture is the one individual who can almost guarantee your reelection. Who was it that said, "Don't complain about the farmer if you have food on your table"? Whoever it was understood that the Secretary of Agriculture should be able to keep people happy by keeping the entire country fed—often and well. Farm issues may not be very sexy, but that doesn't mean that they shouldn't be a priority in your administration. (Or at least somewhere in your top 100 things to address.) Hungry people get cranky and don't respond well to anyone, especially the President. People love food and if your administration can provide them with tons of food—preferably those deliciously high in fat and/or sugar—they will love you too. Let's be honest, fat people are always laughing, whereas skinny people always seem pissed at the world. Enough banter, on to the questions.

190. Which of the following innovative programs would you consider as a way to bring our country back to contentment and self-satisfaction?

- ❑**a.** Implement a new food pyramid that guarantees 4,200 calories a day.
- ❑**b.** Renew efforts to make people aware of the dangers of eating fish and fowl. Make sure people

know that eliminating them by devouring them will not prevent a pandemic.

> **NOTE** Use keywords in your program like red meat, cheese, chocolate ice cream, et cetera.

- ❑**c.** Make marijuana legal and designate specific abandoned inner-city playgrounds to grow and readily make this product available to anyone who wants to enjoy life a bit. Create these gardens of pleasure in the same vein as the "Victory Gardens." (They may have been "war gardens," but it was still an attempt to make this country a better place to live.)
- ❑**d.** Exercise the little used "right of eminent domain" as sanctioned by implication in a phrase in the Fifth Amendment to the US Constitution: ". . . Act and seize all farmland that is not owned by US Citizens." (Well, something along those lines.) Convert the existing buildings into minimum-security prisons and use that population to work the farms. This free labor will allow the government to produce USDA Prime beef at a low price. Then everyone can enjoy the wonderful taste of high-fat-content prime rib.

GO ON TO THE NEXT PAGE

NOTE

When introducing any of the above programs, the only requirement will be to fill out a short form that entitles them to a lifetime of benefits. This application can also include a voter registration section that is limited only to your party. Consider adding a "proxy vote" section. People shouldn't have to worry about missing an election while they're in the backyard "having a smoke" and enjoying life.

191. If you were going to cut costs in the Department of Agriculture, which of the following choices would you consider?

- ❑ **a.** Have the government buy lots of barren and unwanted land. Then use the subsidies you get for not growing wheat to support food banks in needy communities.
- ❑ **b.** Pay all the workers in state parks, preserves, and on Native American reservations to secretly turn those areas into rental properties. Then use the money you make on the rental fees to explore for oil. There probably wouldn't be any oil, but it would create lots of jobs and you could tax those wages in order to support national security programs.

❑c. Ask all family farmers with daughters to marry them off to traveling salesmen. This would help alleviate the terrible burden of supporting a young woman who serves no purpose except, perhaps, to be the butt of bad jokes.

CHECK YOUR WORK AND MAKE SURE YOU DIDN'T MAKE A FOOL OF YOURSELF.

TAKE A DEEP BREATH AND CONTINUE ON TO THE NEXT CHAPTER.

DIPLOMATIC IMMUNITY

(Or, When I Retire I Will . . .)

CHAPTER NINE

192. Before you make any foreign policy appointments, you'll need to decide how you see the "place" in which we all exist. How would you describe that place?

- ❑**a.** My city.
- ❑**b.** My country.
- ❑**c.** My world.
- ❑**d.** My earth.

WOW, DID YOU find that question a little heady? Are you thinking, "What do they expect me to say? Is this another trick? Are they looking for global perspective? Do they want my address for mailing? Do they think I am more qualified to be an astronaut than President?" Get over yourself. We thought you needed a break and we didn't want you to lose the big MO by a lapse in the Q&A process.

POTUS Training Exercise #17

Like the song says, "You're sitting on top of the world." Okay, the song says, "I'm sitting on top of the world." But I'm not taking the test, so picture yourself sitting on the top of a globe. Yes, it will have to be a big steady globe or you will hurt yourself. And it probably should be an electronic globe that identifies all the countries in the world—along with their national songs and the products they export—so you won't have to be embarrassed by asking a foreign service officer for guidance.

Back to the globe. You have decided that since the United States of America is the greatest country in the world, it must be perceived that way. It has to become THE destination for any pursuit of happiness. The only way to accomplish this is to select ambassadors who can carry that image and message to other nations. "Who should

I select to be the ambassadors," you ask yourself, "and how I should select them?" (It's a separate thought, we just don't have enough space for too many thoughts)

193. Please choose the answer that comes closest to the way you would make the selection.

- ❑**a.** Use the motion picture industry as a reference guide. Didn't Marlon Brando do well in *The Ugly American*? Or, how good was Brad Pitt when his quest took him to Tibet? J-Lo would be perfect for Greece (for obvious reasons). Perhaps Snoop Dogg for Haiti (no one can understand anything they say either). Jay Leno or Jerry Lewis for France (they need to lighten up). Pamela Anderson for China (that would put a smile on their faces).
- ❑**b.** For those hard to deal with countries, select members of the Outlaws and Hell's Angels motorcycle gangs to convince them that we are serious when we make demands. Their official mode of transportation would be their Harleys with sidecars. The sidecars are necessary to always have their "bitches" along for the ride.

GO ON TO THE NEXT PAGE

(This would especially irritate the Muslims.) Their primary mission would be to set up "counterculture" organizations and at the same time overthrow the current regimes.

❑c. Do what all your predecessors have done. Appoint all those large contributors to the country of their choice. But just how many Chinese, Israelis, and Sicilians can you appoint to one country?

194. What assets should be the most important when appointing your ambassadors? Would you consider any of the following to be important qualities? A simple yes or no will be sufficient to let us know your state of mind.

❑a. Those who have shown an incredible ability to change the way people think, such as gurus, shamans, cult leaders, grand marshals, and television weathermen.

❑b. Extremely obese, ugly, malformed, egoistical individuals who have narcissistic personalities and would clearly exemplify the "Ugly American." It's a "birds of a feather stick together" kind of approach.

❑c. People who live in the past. Particularly ones who have studied the war of 1776, the Civil War, and the Louisiana Purchase. These individuals have incredible insights into capitalism and how democracy comes into play as an integral part of any potential growth.

❑**d.** Past speechwriters who have had their original statements changed at the last minute to convey a more simplistic solution for our future. Originals like, "Who cares?" "Not in my lifetime," "Safe sex is good but can be a lot better with drugs," or the most famous one, "It's not my blood and guts that I'm spilling. Screw 'em."

195. It's difficult to make decisions about who should be an ambassador, so you decide to give them all a "look-see," and assemble all of them in one theatre. Before the meeting, you receive some startling news. There are more ambassadors than countries! This wasn't always the case, but since so many countries went through regime changes and adopted new names, you learn there are more names than places. Whenever a country was renamed, a new embassy was built and a new ambassador was sent over—without any thought for the ambassadors who were already there serving the old country. Some countries now have two ambassadors and two embassies. There is even a rumor that several countries have three embassies and three ambassadors in residence. There has never been an oversight committee for placing ambassadors, so now you are left with this terrible mess. To rectify this confusing situation, which of the following programs would you consider?

❑**a.** When all the ambassadors are assembled, you make your entrance while "Hail to the Chief"

GO ON TO THE NEXT PAGE

plays in the background. At that time, all will rise. When you get to the podium, the first thing you do is ask everyone to remain standing and look underneath their seat. Anyone who finds a sticker with a country's name on it is allowed to sit down. Those who remain standing should leave and turn in their identification badges on the way out. Now you can get down to business, and since there was no prearranged seating, you won't be accused of playing favorites.

❑ **b.** Place ambassadors by the size of their country. For instance, Monaco should only have a quarter of an ambassador, which means that its ambassador can also cover three other small countries. Russia would probably need four full-time ambassadors and several part-time ambassadors. Additionally, a country with no government needs no ambassador. Countries like Somalia, Bali, and France are just a few.

NOTE

There is one exception to this size-placement program. Our largest embassy, with a staff of over two thousand, can be found in Iraq, where there are only 25 million people (and that number is being drastically reduced on a daily basis). The best thing you can do with that situation is to never bring it up.

❑c. Any ambassadors on Social Security should be removed immediately. You can also remove all those individuals who have handicaps. (You certainly don't want any "gimps" destroying our "all-American" image.)

❑d. In order to maintain a strong foreign service, it may be necessary to allow underpaid ambassadors to own and operate gifts shops in their embassies. (As an added bonus, they can sell autographed pictures of you and other memorabilia.) Be careful of letting them open up delis—you don't want to be selling hot pork sandwiches in Afghanistan.

196. One of the most challenging and difficult undertakings any President has to confront is to find a way to control the thinking of the leaders and people of other nations. And, of course, to get them to understand that the American Way is the only way. (Maybe we do need an Agency for International Understanding.) What would you do to ensure that the US is always in control?

❑a. Continue with the Favored Nations Act—if they don't want to play by your rules, they can't play at all.

❑ **b.** Send enough US troops to make a point about what is the right way (aka the American Way) to do things.

> **NOTE**
>
> Send *just* enough troops to make a point, but not enough to have to support them in any real, essential way.

❑ **c.** Sponsor a sale where you sell products from other countries, but only if they start to think the way we do. Then share the profits as an example of what they could gain if they relinquish their own culture.

197. While Americans love their fine country, they often go to other countries to vacation. Unfortunately, there are often demonstrations, chaos, and rioting in other countries. (Yes, even countries with those fancy-schmancy vacation resorts that spoiled Americans adore.) Since you never want Americans to be disturbed (especially if they are on nonrefundable vacations), you've chosen a diplomatic team that can quell the disturbance and protect American lives. What would you advise your diplomats to do if there's a conflict that involves machine guns blazing or apparent

weapons of mass destruction? Choose the best alternative from the following choices.

- ❑**a.** Run like a bat out of hell and protect yourself. You are no good to any discounted tourist if you are dead.
- ❑**b.** Call the embassy Public Affairs Officer (PAO) and see if they have any television network contacts. There's a good chance that the riot is being choreographed for the media and the PAO may know how to turn it off.
- ❑**c.** Join in the fun. This may be your only opportunity to really get to know foreign opinion makers and religious leaders. At the very least, you'll get some phone numbers for next time.
- ❑**d.** Call the embassy visa office and hotels.com immediately, and make sure no one from the country in conflict has permission or, worse, a ticket to come to the US. Remember, your real job is to do whatever is necessary to keep this bad behavior abroad.

198. As you know, once you've completed this test, it'll be evaluated by us. But we forgot to mention that we're also forwarding your test to our forensic psychiatric staff in order to determine what events have driven your desire to become President. To help them verify that you are on the right track, please choose the event that is most similar to

GO ON TO THE NEXT PAGE

your own personal Presidential epiphany from the following choices.

- ❑**a.** When you thought that ex-President Harry S. Truman's famous quote, "The buck stops here," meant, "Gee, that's a lot of bucks, I'll never be poor again."
- ❑**b.** While holding your breath at a frat party, you had an awesome vision (brought on by oxygen deprivation). You saw yourself sitting in the Oval Office, surrounded by a bevy of beautiful interns.
- ❑**c.** While playing *Monopoly* as a child you thought, "If I were President, I could have as many 'get out of jail free' cards as I wanted."
- ❑**d.** During your college years, and before getting your hearing aid, you always answered "yes" when the professor asked, "Are you present"? You thought the teacher was asking if you wanted to be President and just assumed it was your destiny.
- ❑**e.** Your dream was to become a great writer. Since you didn't have any talent in that department, you decided that it was easier to become President, hire a ghostwriter, and write a memoir, which would automatically become a bestseller.

- ❑ **f.** After discovering late in life that you possessed deep homosexual tendencies, you became obsessed with the idea of all the President's men.
- ❑ **g.** All you ever wanted to do was to ride in the backseat of a limo.
- ❑ **h.** Actually, you have little desire to become President, but your spouse has worn you down over the years with the incessant obsession to have her own bowling alley or redecorate the White House.

199. It's never too early to begin planning what you'll do after you leave office. Of course, you think it will go on forever, but even if (by the grace of the electorate) you're granted eight years, it'll be over before you know it. To help with developing your plans for the future, please match the following careers with the former Presidents who are now involved with them.

- ❑ **a.** Supervising one of the most massive underwater tunnel projects known to man and building a four-lane tunnel between Key West and Havana.
- ❑ **b.** Managing a nonprofit organization to explore the use of chickens as fossil fuel.
- ❑ **c.** A movie mogul who produces silent black-and-white documentaries about what really goes on in the government behind closed doors.

GO ON TO THE NEXT PAGE

❑**d.** Purchasing Neverland and turning it into a political training arena, complete with courses on how to maintain weapons, charge-and-retreat philosophies, the art of picking pockets, managing health-care organizations, and speechwriting with spiritual healers.

200. Everyone knows the job of President is the hardest in the world, but what is the second hardest job out there?

❑**a.** Troop commander in Iraq.
❑**b.** Garbage detail in NYC.
❑**c.** Mormon missionary in Damascus.
❑**d.** Stem cell researcher at Oral Roberts University.
❑**e.** A pimp.

201. The media will provide you with many opportunities to spend an enormous amount of time in the homes of the people who elected you (they will see you more than they will see their own families). If there were a reality show called *The President Speaks*, how would you sign off from the broadcast, night after night after night?

❑**a.** Sometimes you eat the bear, and sometimes the bear eats you.
❑**b.** Be careful out there.
❑**c.** Don't let the bed bugs bite.
❑**d.** Good night and good luck.

CHECK YOUR WORK AND MAKE SURE YOU DIDN'T MAKE A FOOL OF YOURSELF.

TAKE A DEEP BREATH AND CONTINUE ON TO THE NEXT CHAPTER.

THE RESULTS ARE IN . . .

PUT DOWN YOUR PENS.

The test is over.

FIRST OFF, ARE you wondering why there were 201 questions when we clearly stated there were going to be 200? No, it wasn't for extra credit. We didn't play by the rules. Did you forget that this is a test about Presidential politics? There are no rules except to win.

This leads perfectly into how we will score your answers. You did spend a significant amount of time on this and you probably think it's the least we can do. We did say you could send your answers to soyouthinkyoucanbepresident.com (the web site) but did we mention "wellwe'llbethejudgeofthat"? Of course, some objective yet incredibly intuitive person or persons has to be . . . so it might as well be the test crafters.

In order for you to learn your score immediately, we hope that you purchased the electronically enhanced pens that were available at the same place you made your purchase. Remove the eraser from the pen, hold it over every question, and then place it in your ear. The scores that will be determined are based on numerous sensors we placed in your pen. The device will transmit the answers you have provided instantly, as they were programmed to read your written answers and evaluate them. They will also evaluate the manner in which you held the instrument, the amount of wavering or smoothness of flow in your writing, the weight of the pen tip exerted on the paper, your blood pressure, breathing, and the temperature of stored urine.

You should receive both the answer to the questions and an aggregate score. If you haven't given a correct answer in the first four pages you'll receive an instruction to break the pen in half, remove the eraser from your ear, and quietly leave the room.

If you didn't purchase the special pen, shame on you. It makes more work for us and we're not happy about it. However, you can submit your answers to the web site. In order to download your score it's a good idea to enter your Social Security number as your user name and a valid credit card number with expiration date as your password. The score you receive will be based solely on the way you answered the questions. There is no scoring curve, because you're really not competing with anyone but yourself.

If you scored 80% to 100%: Start taking lessons on how to play "Hail to the Chief" on the musical instrument of your choosing. Hire a choreographer so you won't look foolish at all of the Inaugural Balls.

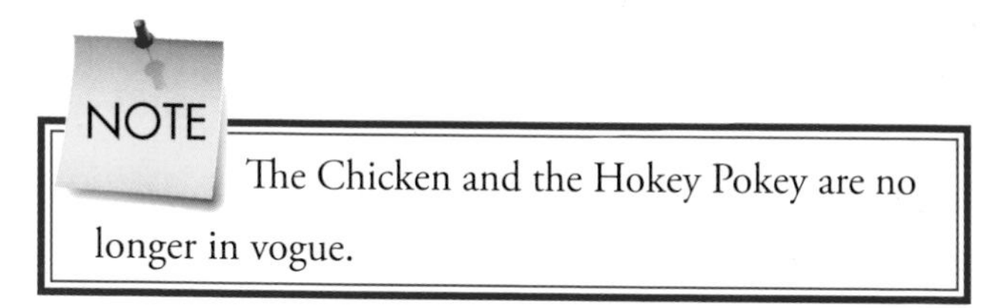

NOTE

The Chicken and the Hokey Pokey are no longer in vogue.

Enroll your spouse in as many extreme makeover clinics as possible. The most important is the verbal control clinic, otherwise known as "when to keep your mouth shut." Start dispersing your assets to as many hidden accounts and offshore banks as soon as possible. You should also start spending many hours looking at yourself in the mirror repeating, "I love you, I love you."

50% to 79%: You have a fifty-fifty chance to win (most test takers and actual Presidential candidates score in this range). In the meantime, keep up with your continuing education programs.

0% to 50%: Focus on the adage "I could have been a contender," and don't allow yourself to become clinically depressed. You did the best you could, it just wasn't good enough. Acceptance of "you are who you are" can be very healing.

If you scored in the top 20 percent we can, for a minimal fee, forward your results to your choice of national political parties.

If you scored in the mediocre range we can, for a somewhat larger fee, not forward your results to national political parties.

If you scored in the bottom range and you come from a wealthy family, you may have your score changed. For this service we have long-term financing available at a reasonable rate.

If you are thinking we violated your civil rights then you should look closer at the Waiver of the Freedom of Information statement you signed as part of your test.

The actual ANSWER KEY can be found on the web site:

www.soyouthinkyoucanbepresident.com

PRESIDENTIAL GLOSSARY

A few helpful phrases to learn before you become the next President of the United States.

Absentee Voting: As in "I don't remember seeing anyone in that booth but the levers were pulled."

Affirmative Action: Being acutely aware of the melting ice cap and the prediction that oceans will rise almost twelve feet in the next thirty-five years. That height increase will cover almost 4,300 miles of American's coast line. The Army Corps of Engineers have been tasked to build levee systems that will protect coastal land and cities. This project will take 125 years to complete.

Beltway: While most people in the news and on their way to and from their homes think of this as a mental state, we think of it as what it is—a road that surrounds

Washington, D.C. The traffic on this road, much like the actions in the government, is always in a traffic jam. And like the mental state some think it represents, there are numerous accidents because people don't pay attention to the road they have chosen to take. We would simply advise you to tighten your beltways. You could be in for the ride of your life.

Bipartisan: A derivative of Bipolarism. Although not as profound, it has the same effect on someone's personality. One goes to sleep confident about the day and wakes up to the morning news a nervous wreck. In addition, one never knows on what side of the bed, or in whose bed, they'll wind up.

Chad: The offspring of chafes. Can also be a small punched-out piece of paper with a hidden code used in contests. If you match the code at a national drawing, you'll become President. Chads are often used in eye examinations to determine the ability to see things that don't exist. Unknown until 2000, the chad is a defective Y chromosome that develops into an obsession to run for the Presidency. Research reveals that this defective chromosome is passed on from father to son. Chads can also be chafers: a couple who intentionally have male offspring to maintain a control over a large population. Used as a noun, chafing is the art of making chads.

Constituent: A voter who has spent a great deal of time conning and "stiting." This person, who is busy "uenting" often authorizes another to act as agent. Therefore constituents are often considered to be not in their right minds or "stuck on dumb."

DeBait: A challenge, covert operation, or news story used to entice someone to take the hook.

DeBaiter: As in, the dumb ass took it and now he has to open his big mouth.

DeBaiting: Removing the hook by filleting the debaiter from head to toe.

Ethical: Being morally obligated to your beliefs. And if you enjoy being self-centered, selfish, and not giving a damn about others, that's your right. Only you can be the judge. Actually, many people would consider being a judge far more important than being the President. It's certainly a longer term.

Exit Poll: Standing at the exit of a voting place and, as the voters exit, asking them whom they voted for. Then giving that information to an organization that will use the data to give to the media so they can make zillions in advertising dollars being first with information. No one really cares if the voters tell the truth, as long as someone is first.

Foreign Affairs: A little known perk about which only Secret Service agents are aware. It's their responsibility to arrange for young ambassadresses or ambassadrettes (the dress thing sounds so sexist) to meet with the President to lay out and demonstrate cultural differences. If pleasing, these ambassadrets could be appointed to the World Bank to continue to give their expertise to foreign heads of states.

Hard Money: A candidate with a low approval rating who is soliciting people for donations to the next campaign. That's really hard money.

Hearts and Minds: While this expression has come to be synonymous with winning over the electorate, its derivation is based on one of the main components of a formula discovered and used by Count Dracula. It's based on a theory that if you grab someone by the throat and sink your teeth into them there will be an enormous loss of blood and their hearts will surely stop. Then by a simple transfusion of your own blood they will forever answer only to your whims. Its success today, like so many other issues, is totally dependent on Congress's ability to pass legislation. In this case, HR 2468: a bill that will waive the requirement to have a licensed medical technician perform blood transfusions.

Hybrid: A person who tries to participate in electoral politics but can never decide which person or party gets the most out of an issue. While it is true that they are often well intentioned, they are also often confused and, as the word implies, flying about as high as a brid.

Interim: Not to be confused with intern. Both are temporary, however one is an appointment and one is an appointee who, if you are not discreet, can become ever lasting.

Intern: An individual who is always willing to be helpful and for the honor of being close to power will "in turn" provide the elected official with lots of extracurricular activity—especially during periods when a spouse is away. The intern should be selected based on the same criteria on which one would select models for publication in the Victoria Secret's catalog or *Men's Fitness*.

Katrina: The half-sister of Medusa. You won't turn to stone if you gaze at her, but you will experience an enormous sense of being lost, followed by an uncontrollable desire to curl up and whine, "Why me?"

Lame Duck: Many people think this is only one ineffective species that by law is really not able to do anything, but many people are incorrect. There are several kinds of lame ducks with distinctly different problems.

- **Left-wing lame duck:** A duck with a virus that makes it impossible for the duck to circle right. It keeps circling left, only to end up diving into the ground.
- **Right-wing lame duck:** Same duck, same virus, however, it keeps climbing to the right until it can't get any higher and then explodes into thin air.
- **Simple lame duck:** An ordinary duck with no virus that just keeps flying around in circles and keeps ending up in the same place without any hope of ever advancing in a straight line.

Line Item Veto: Allows the President to remove any item on any bill that would benefit the opposing party. Because he wouldn't have to discuss this removal, it would create animosity for a rival politician among his constituents, who will come to believe that he is doing nothing for them.

Ombudsmen: An obscure small group of guru types who lead meditation sessions for politicians who have strayed off the beaten path. Originally, they were referred to as Bud Men, due to the large amount of beer they consumed during these gatherings. However, over the years that name changed to Ombudsmen because of their unusual chant

during their sessions: Ommmmmm, ommmmmm, omm-mmmm.

OpEd: An article that is published and read by "OpEd-Ers." Normally a group formed to honor and pay homage to syndicated writers who attached a redeemable coupon to their columns that can be used to buy the next edition, thereby building a following that will be used to renegotiate their next contract for more money.

Outsourcing: A covert program where individuals are hired in foreign countries to learn a trade. After their apprenticeships have been financed, they immigrate back to the United States and are placed in abandoned industrial centers. Here they develop products similar to the ones they worked on abroad. This not only helps the US economy, it undermines the foreign economy and insures a constant supply of low-wage workers who have no idea they are even in West Virginia.

Oval Office: The President's office in the White House. It is a unique shape. Most people do not know that the design was copied from large corporate office tables. In the corporation, the object of an oval table was to disguise the real person in charge. If there was no head of the table, mistakes could never be blamed on the person who sat at the head. In the White House it is a way to disguise a power play and eliminate the slowest to respond. There are never enough seats for all the people invited, so meetings become a game of musical chairs. The last one standing is out.

Permanent Residence: A special statute enacted in 1955 allowing all those being held at Area 51 (regardless of their home country, age, religion, or breakfast of choice) to become permanent residents. However, they were subsequently transferred to Guantanamo Bay, Cuba, in 2003. That's the last time they were ever heard from.

Phil A. Buster: A distant relative of Fat E. Arbuckle who, after becoming a US Senator, set a record for never voting on a single issue. He spent most of his time with other old politicians sitting around, smoking cigars, drinking whisky, and doing nothing other than killing time. Hence they became Phil A. Busters!

Pocket Veto: A veiled threat or a solicitation. When the President sends a message to the Congress, his security confronts a member and whispers in his or her ear, "Here's something the President wants to say: 'Don't make me use this.'" The security person needs to be standing with a hand in his pocket. It does take a little choreography, but there is never a doubt that a message is being sent.

Political Correctness: The art of never doing, saying, or thinking anything that will offend or embarrass anyone. This includes but is not limited to references about body parts (small breasts, no ass, cellulite-challenged, weight, baldness, or color of the skin). One way to avoid being accused of insensitivity is to practice "mum's the word." Political correctness must be practiced when speaking to the media, bloggers, and registered voters. The only time you do not need to be a practicing political corrector is when you find yourself (try never to lose yourself) surrounded by a group of nonvoters. Then feel free to say whatever the hell you want. Here's how to have some "politi-correct" fun that might result in a victory. Go to where the opposition gathers and introduce yourself as a member of their party. Tell them just the way you think it is—use racial slurs, gender bash, ridicule physical and mental defects, show no compassion for crippled and maimed malcontent degenerates. You are almost guaranteed to swing potential voters to your party.

Political Novice: An aspiring candidate who thinks the President actually carries a wallet.

Political Parties (Democrats or Republicans): Political parties exist so that people can attend without having any information or paying an admission fee. It's called a party because you can stand around with a drink, pontificating about your problems and whom to blame for them. While some of the stances on issues do differ, the lines (unless the person is a right-wing lunatic or a left-wing wacko) are never blurred by facts. (This kind of party, like a fraternity, is certainly a great example of the "herd instinct" or "lemmings to the sea." It provides a way to belong to anything just once in one's life. What does it mean to belong to a Grand Old Party? We know there is a DOPE but is there a DOP?)

If you are a member of the left wing, you believe:

a. Tree hugging is better then petting to climax.
b. Al Gore picked the wrong ties to match his jeans.
c. Organic gardening is the profession to which you have always aspired.
d. There is a right-wing conspiracy controlling everything you see.

If you are a member of the right wing, you believe:

a. There are no bad guns, only bad shots.
b. George Bush Sr. never needed to know the cost of a loaf of bread.
c. Being a teacher at Bob Jones University is the profession to which you have always aspired.
d. There is a left-wing conspiracy trying to destroy everything you believe in.

Politics: Is synonymous with infomercial. Also considered the genesis for propaganda. The art of making people, who have no clue what you are talking about, become believers. The word has an interesting history. When the first settlers came to America, hungry, disillusioned, and wanting money, they discovered they could rapidly acquire massive amounts of valuable articles of comfort by trading with the Native Americans. In a short time they were so good at trading that they became viewed as gods. So they decided they may as well act as gods. They had totem poles carved in their own images, which were distributed all over and used as a way to confiscate land. There was one tribe, however, that was quite smart. They were called the Pole Ticks. (Their name came from their ability to eliminate disease-carrying ticks by chasing them through the briar and bramble patches and beating them with long slender poles.) Decades passed and the settlers amassed considerable land, built places of worship, and enlisted many converts, but they did not take care of their health. The Pole Ticks continued to maintain their independence and eliminate disease. Eventually, many of the settlers got very sick and could not go to town meetings. Hence, they were forced to turn to the Pole Ticks to maintain the local governments.

Polling/Pollster: A questioning or canvassing of persons selected at random to obtain information or opinions. The pollster who collects the most positive opinions for his candidate earns the right to be his press secretary. Hint: If you want that position, never, but never, write down any negative opinions. Like blogging, what in the hell is that and who really reads that stuff? A million people? What about the other 290 million that don't read it because they are unsure if it's a porno site or a rerun of *The Twilight Zone*?

President's Cup: A device worn over the genitals to protect against losing the family jewels. Also known as headgear to staff members whose sole purpose in life is to protect his behind and the parts in the immediate vicinity.

Presidential Pardon: A special power the President has to forgive foolish behavior. Instances include:

- "Ooops, sorry about that, I always get airsick, I'll have the aide get you something clean to wear."
- "I didn't mean any harm, I truly thought I saw a lizard run up your leg."
- "Honest, I didn't know my pocket had a large tear in it when I asked you to reach in and take out my keys."
- "Let me make myself clear. When I said, 'Who Cares?' I really was looking for an answer."
- "My Fellow Americans, I humbly ask for your forgiveness for my inability to act when we were attacked. I was trying to figure out whom to attack when I was told we were being attacked. I thought the attack was from

a country that we had planned to attack eventually. I began praying and I thought a little drinking couldn't hurt. That's when I saw God, and he approved of my reluctance to make a quick decision. I truly believe that we must not question God's good judgment."

Pro-Choice: If you are pro-choice, you:

a. Know that God is on your side in the Northeast and on the West Coast.

b. Have no idea what it means but you know it's not specific to any issue—so you can choose to do pretty much anything you want to do. No heavy lifting, no cleaning, no catering to the needs of others, and certainly no windows.

c. Realize that no one is pro-no-choice, so you can wile away the hours feeling good about the issue until there is a new Supreme Court in place.

Pro-Life: If you are pro-life, you:

a. Wake up in the morning with the urge to adopt an infant that belongs to your next-door neighbor.

b. Go to sleep at night with the knowledge that you can bomb a planned parenthood clinic with simple kitchen supplies.

c. Realize that no one is pro-death, but you've lucked into some great rhetoric.

Pundit: This description is derived from the two words pun and ditz. If used correctly it means someone who cannot tell a real joke and has difficulty thinking clear and cogent thoughts.

Soft Money: By using the information gathered by the US National Security Agency (or a credit card company) about wealthy people with Middle Eastern heritage or people whose political party is not in power, it is possible to capture pin numbers. Then, armed with all this top-secret information, you send a platoon of volunteers all over the world making withdrawals and buying designer clothes. Another name often used is "Easy Money."

Special Investigator: A eunuch (this might be an insult but not determined with any malice) with a law degree who has been trained in the use of night-vision goggles and infrared-sensor equipment. He usually has a fondness for voyeurism, but this is not necessarily a requirement. He might also just have good friends who have been formerly with the Secret Service or the French Foreign Legion.

Testing the Water: A political phrase used when someone has no money but might have natural resources. In this case, however, it is used as a measure of your ability to make sound judgments. If you took the time to take a surprise trivia test, instead of leaping right into the actual

Presidential examination, the test crafters believe that the pattern would not change. And for all your years in office, you will do nothing more than find ways to waste time. This is not good thing for the nation. Please close your test, take a time out in whatever corner you can find, and think about how you are going to make reparations for what you've done.

NOTE

Money or a promise for a lucrative lobbying contract would be a good start.

Treaties: Usually some pieces of paper indicating a humiliating arrangement between two countries at war, which would never last because no entity wants to be considered a loser. It can be used as "Hey little girl, want some treaties?" Which is usually more of a lasting commitment.

Veto: An action or mechanism used to insure the President's policies are never impeded. As in, "Tell them I'll call Veto if I have to."

Voting Machine: A person who can register and vote in all precincts in their city at least twice.

Whip: Usually a small rubber replica of a whip with the words "The floggings will continue until the bill is passed" imprinted upon it. This is used to remind party members of their obligations.

White House Conjugal Visits: Although this sounds a little like something that happens in a prison, it is quite the opposite. No one ever wants to leave. This is a little known perk that allows the President or the First Lady to offer large donors [sic] an opportunity to spend a night or two in one of a few designated bedrooms. They are sometimes referred to as congeniality visits, but we don't know what goes on behind closed doors.

ACKNOWLEDGMENTS

The authors gratefully thank the following:

Iris's mom, Rose, who never knew what she was doing but got to have lunch in the White House Mess.

Clay's mom, Mildred, who liked being called Geraldine and wondered when Clay learned to write.

Tom Herman, our dear friend and lawyer, who worked tirelessly to make sure we didn't make foolish mistakes or lose too much money.

Tony Lyons, who saw the potential of publishing a humorous political test in a Presidential election year.

Editorial assistants Junessa Viloria and Alaina Sudeith, and Brando Skyhorse, our talented and insightful "think out of the box" editor, who was able to make sense of all our nonsense and craft a book about which we are thrilled beyond all the words we used and he eliminated.

The wonderful people who understand how important it is to have a sense of humor about such a serious topic and were courageous enough to comment on a book that makes fun of a subject they love: Senator John Kerry, Newt Gingrich, P.J. O'Rourke, Dave Barry, Mike Peters, Tom Oliphant, Donna E. Shalala, Senator Bob Kerrey, Randy Wayne Wright, Steve Daley, Dr. Allan Jacobson, and Robert John Burck (aka The Naked Cowboy).

To Soozie and Jeff MacNelly, who brought us together because they saw the possibilities in a collaboration between two incredibly wacky friends.

And to all the friends (thousands, but we only care about twenty—you know who you are) who have been there from the first Presidential campaign we were involved in to the last one we ridiculed.

Finally, Clay wishes to thank that "Washington VIP" who called Iris while she was visiting his store. After overhearing an absolutely intriguing conversation, he said, "Iris, who in the hell are you?" Once discovering her credentials he asked her, "Why don't you run for President?" She replied, "I couldn't pass the test!"

ABOUT THE AUTHORS

IRIS BURNETT is a veteran of the political process. Her experience with Presidential elections includes key roles in eight campaigns and a presidential appointment as director of security for the 1980 Democratic Convention. To this day she is the only woman to have served in this capacity at a national political convention. In the post-election realm of politics, she has been a political advisor to two presidents and numerous other elected officials.

Burnett served as chief of staff at the former United States Information Agency (USIA), where she supervised personnel and presided over a budget of one billion dollars. She was also a liaison to the White House, the State Department, Congress, foreign embassies, and various corporate partners and public service organizations. During her tenure at USIA, Burnett helped to create the White House Women's Office and the President's Interagency Council for Women. She served as an official delegate to the United Nations Commission on the Status of Women and to the U.N. Fourth World Conference on Women in Beijing, where she directed communications for the Congressional delegation and the White House.

Burnett then served as the Senior Vice President of Corporate Communications, Public Affairs, and Government Relations for the Sci-Fi Channel and USA Network. There she developed "Erase the Hate," an award-winning national campaign to promote understanding and respect for individual differences in a diverse society.

Burnett has demonstrated a lifelong commitment to supporting women's rights. In addition to her various philanthropic accomplishments at USIA, Burnett has served as chairman of the board and was a co-founder of Count Me In for Women's Economic Independence. This non-profit organization was the world's first online micro-lending organization.

She is also a former professor at American University's School of Communication. She firmly believes that no one but Clay should have the same job for more than four years.

Currently, Burnett is the president of Kai Productions, which specializes in advocacy and communication strategy.

Her ongoing philanthropic efforts involve serving on the Board of Directors at the Erase the Hate Foundation, and on the National Advisory Board at Count Me In for Women's Economic Independence. She has also received a presidential appointment to the Board of Governors of the United Services Organization (USO). She is the author of *Schlepper! A Mostly True Tale of Presidential Politics* and the executive producer of *The Gefilte Fish Chronicles*, a documentary about family, tradition and celebration.

CLAY GREAGER swears by the philosophy that one must live in accordance with one's own desires, not the expectations of others. Combined with his lifelong love of the written word, Clay's philosophy of life has led him to create a thriving business and write several books about his war experiences. His books include *The Last Flight Out*; *A State of Mind; Key West, Where the Sun Rises Just for You*; and *A License to Dream*.

Greager, who grew up working the farms and coal mines of Pennsylvania, is a two-tour Vietnam veteran. He spent most of his military career as a helicopter gunner, but was himself gunned down by the enemy while on a mission. When rescued, Greager became the subject of a famous combat photo known as "Thousand Yard Stare." His experiences in Vietnam taught him what it is like to face death, how to cope with losing friends, and how to deal with people who refuse to accept those with opposing

political beliefs. When the war ended he moved to Key West, Florida.

In the 1970s Greager opened a store called Last Flight Out. The name comes from a story about the town as it was before it became the tourist haven it is today. In those days, the Air Sunshine airline, frequently called "Air Sometimes" due to its unreliability, was the only way to reach Key West. Visitors then, like now, spent a great deal of time drinking in the bars. Whenever the bartenders were ready to close up for the evening, instead of saying "last call" they would say "last flight out," at which time everyone would relocate to the twenty-four-hour airport bar. Since neither the patrons nor the Air Sunshine pilots ever wanted leave the party, the last flight out of Key West was often cancelled. In addition to starting up his new store, Greager began to revisit his old passion of writing. He began telling his stories and sharing the experiences that had changed his life.

Greager is continually helping people to find their way in life and experience as much as possible. Although he believes that anything north of the Mile 5 marker must be Georgia, his goal is "to have as many chapters in his life as possible."

ANSWER KEY

As we just said several pages earlier, the actual ANSWER KEY can be found on the website. We hate it when we have to repeat ourselves, but we need to insure all our potential POTUSes have been properly briefed. Besides, we weren't sure how else to segue into these additional instructions:

- To receive your score in a language other than English, click on the flag of the corresponding country at the bottom of the page.
- To receive an encoded score, download the appropriate file located near the bottom of the page.
- To receive a key to *unlock* your encoded score, hit the refresh button twice.
- To receive an audio score, click on both the flag of your choosing and the ear horn symbol within .5 seconds of one another, or hold your mouse over the finance symbol for six seconds.
- If you receive a laughing clown picture instead of an actual score, well, you can figure that one out yourself.

While checking your score, remember that the President can never, even under the direst of circumstances, appear confused, aggravated, or dismayed. So be brave and go forth to:

www.soyouthinkyoucanbepresident.com

NOTES

NOTES

SO YOU THINK YOU CAN BE PRESIDENT?

SO YOU THINK YOU CAN BE PRESIDENT?

NOTES